HOW TO

Unfeel the Dead

NEW AND SELECTED FICTIONS

D1453602

ALSO BY LANCE OLSEN

NOVELS
Live from Earth
Tonguing the Zeitgeist
Burnt
Time Famine
Freaknest
Girl Imagined by Chance
10:01
Nietzsche's Kisses
Anxious Pleasures
Head in Flames
Calendar of Regrets
Theories of Forgetting

SHORT STORIES
My Dates with Franz
Scherzi, I Believe
Sewing Shut My Eyes
Hideous Beauties

NONFICTION
Ellipse of Uncertainty
Circus of the Mind in Motion
William Gibson
Lolita: A Janus Text
Rebel Yell: A Short Guide to Fiction Writing
Architectures of Possibility: After Innovative Writing
[[there.]]

HOW TO
Unfeel the Dead
NEW AND SELECTED FICTIONS

lance olsen

Teksteditions
Toronto 2014

Editor: Richard Truhlar
Associate editor: Beverley Daurio
Cover image and author photo: Andi Olsen
Cover, composition and page design: Beverley Daurio
Editorial Assistant: Tyler James

2014 2015 2016 2017 2018   5 4 3 2 1

First Edition

CiP Data available for this title.

Paperback: 978-1-55128-180-3
Hardcover: 978-1-55128-181-0

Teksteditions
www.teksteditions.com

Acknowledgements

I am deeply grateful to the John Simon Guggenheim Memorial Foundation and the University of Utah for providing me time to bring this book to fruition. Many thanks as well to Joshua Beckman, David Memmott, Jeffrey Deshell, Larry McCaffery, Ronald Sukenick, and Carlton Mellick for carrying my fiction collections into the world, and to the editors at *Conjunctions, Denver Quarterly, The Literary Review, Marginalia, Mid-American Review, Pleiades*, and *The &Now Awards: The Best Innovative Writing*, where earlier versions of the previously uncollected pieces here first appeared.

Contents

New Fictions
(2004-2013)

for Andi, & all our worlds

And what does skin have to do with autobiography?

— Leigh Gilmore

FROM

My Dates with Franz

(1993)

Two Children Menaced by a Nightingale

IN MAX ERNST'S FAMOUS ASSEMBLAGE the sky is a dark blue strip at the top of the canvas. Then increasingly paler and paler green as it ladders down in layers toward the bright orange-pink outline of the wooden house pasted in the right corner. It finally turns lemon as it nuzzles the orange-pink wall stretching along the grassy lawn toward the vanishing point beyond the classical arch on top of which poises the figure whose left arm is raised like that of the Statue of Liberty. The silhouette of another building rises even farther in the background—nothing really but an ashen stain left and several inches below the center. Dark trees bunch behind another wall, this one cement, which intersects the first near that arch. A gleaming frantic red gate from a doll house swings open across the brown-lacquered frame in the foreground.

But all this is infinitely less interesting than what catches your eye in the middle-ground: the five black-and-white figures in disarray. The small bird hovering at the exact point the green sky melts into yellow. The woman, long black hair fluttering behind her, looking up at the nightingale as she darts beneath it with something—a knife? a baton?—in her hand. The clayish lump that appears to be another female body sprawled at an unnatural arc beside the house. The man in the business suit on the roof, the light-haired child in his arms, fleeing toward the blue button with a red-dot core that might just be the sun.

THE DEAD DAUGHTER

It was the most miserable song I ever heard. I was sitting on the back porch at twilight, watching carbon tetrachloride, lead, and perchloroethylene smear the saffron sky various shades of emerald above the factory when it appeared, a black mouth smiling twenty feet in the air. I rose and began to follow it across the lawn, recollecting memories of events that had never actually occurred to me: the tanned body of the boy, twelve or thirteen, who delivers our meat, naked, his stomach ribbed with muscles, his arms and legs and torso glistening, as he knelt before me on that sunny spring day behind the arch, furry bees humming around us, grinning, nubbing his tongue through his lips (only his tongue wasn't made of skin but of hundreds of flies), which excited me almost as much as the realization that three of his friends were watching us—two more boys and a little bald girl, this last whose skin was metallic and who was not (it slowly reached me) a girl at all but an android with red robotic eyes, and smooth bumps for a nose and breasts, and a stereo speaker for a mouth, from which issued the song of the nightingale that conjured the glittering white shores of Greek islands I had never visited, polychromatic parasols dotting the beach, the fragrance of wine and sea salt and fish in the breeze, water the color of California swimming pools licking the sand, portable radios alive with the song of the nightingale that gave rise to New York City where you can hear excitement at three o'clock any morning in a murky alley amid trash-cans leaking brown banana peels and limp whitish shrimp shells above which, in that one-bedroom apartment where you have to move some-thing else just to move the thing you wanted to move, an underfed boy in his late teens, hair purple, greasy skin cratered and nibbed with acne, plays a guitar whose perpetually joyless chords form the song of the nightingale that offered up the marble interior of a colossal art museum with thousands of floors cluttered with countless sculptures and paintings, one of which, hanging in the shadowy corner of an unnumbered level (its title having accidentally been dropped from the catalog over one hundred years ago), depicts the moment of your death, although you wouldn't be able to rec-ognize this fact even if you knew as much and could locate it (which you didn't and which you can't) because the image that is supposed to represent you is simply a metaphor for you and actually represents someone else.

THE WOMAN, LONG BLACK HAIR FLUTTERING BEHIND HER

In the dream I was falling through the night sky. Human heads rained down around me, bouncing when they thumped against the ground below. A row of Gestapo officers shot at me with pistols. No, machine guns. Bullets slapped into me. At the moment I understood something I can no longer remember understanding, something thunked against my bedroom window. I sat up. Véra, my daughter, screaming. It sounded like an army of ants were stinging her. Outside, the sky was the color of scum on the surface of a pond in August, air filled with the beating of wings. When I tried to rush toward the bird diving at her face, pecking at her eyes, tangling in her hair, a dagger appeared in my hand. Yet somehow instead of rushing at the bird I rushed at Véra. And then her legs became marmalade. Her breasts turned candy-red. Her tunic fell open and I saw she was pregnant. My husband shouted in horror behind me. He swept up Vanya who, groggy, still in her flannel robe speckled with antique lampshades, had just stepped through the front door to find out what all the commotion was about. He began to clamber up the side of the house with Vanya in his arms, shouting at me to stay away, stay away, his voice rich with radio static. An abrupt wind arose. The gate blew open. The sun turned blue.

THE NIGHTINGALE

What's that talisman tacked to your front door? A razor? The stick-shift from a car that hasn't yet been imagined by an engineer now sleeping on a bamboo mat in a white-walled Tokyo flat? Is that really a factory on the horizon, or a temple? A figure with its left arm raised, or another smoke-stack? Why does your house stand on stilts? Why is the sun so low in the sky? Is it the sun? Why are you running? What's that in your hand? Why do you think you can reach me? Why was today the same day as yesterday for you in every respect except for my presence? What were you waiting for before you considered changing? What's the secret you've never shared with each other? Why do you sit on your porch every evening, waiting for darkness? Why did you decide on two children and not three? Two, and not none? Why did you decide to live here, and not there? Build your gate without a fence? Love each other? Agree to say you love each other? Who decided what you would do next? What kind of trees are those through the arch, behind the wall? What comes beyond them? What happens when I'm finished? What happens now?

And now?

THE MAN IN THE BUSINESS SUIT ON THE ROOF

I phoned her like in a bad movie to say I had to have dinner with a client, and then went to dinner with that client's daughter, strawberry hair cropped so close you could see her scalp shine through, five small gold hoops in her left ear, one in her right, lipstick the color of plums, knit dress the same, because, well, because, if I had to say, if I had to put my finger on it, because *gravity*, really, because of the way gravity is like an infection, because the way the skin under your eyes cannot be immunized against it, because the way the buttocks become a kind of joke at a certain stage of one's life, no matter what precautions one takes, no matter how much one attempts to believe that youth ultimately comes down to a state of mind, because there are forces besides gravity, like a certain, I don't know, *aura*, perhaps, that radiates around the woman who has over the years delivered one's children, an aura, if one's content with that word, that declaims that certain events, tactics, are now quite out of bounds, and those other forces, like memory, like the recollection of whole other worlds that seem to have existed a long time ago which the word *middle-aged* merely trivializes, because there is so much that, when voiced, sounds like cliché, and so, yes, I phoned like in a bad movie to say the obvious, and then out to dine with her where, contrary to the projected narrative, we discovered we had remarkably much in common, so much so that it began to hurt, physically, seeing how many things we had to talk about, her hopes having become my memories, events in her life more fascinating to me than anything that had happened recently, not because they might have been fascinating to another person, no, but because they were fascinating in their own right because of the simple fact that they existed, they were *there*, they were so remarkably unlike the events in my life that I couldn't hear enough about them, because, well, the point being, afterward, we went back to her apartment in the city—and again the narrative deviation—did absolutely nothing but talk a little more about what we didn't have in common, which is what we had in common, and then I asked her, I'm embarrassed to admit, if we could just, well, *hug* a little while, nothing else, the kissing business seeming downright anticlimactic at this point, because, if the truth be known, all I wanted to do was feel the press of a new body against mine, which she somehow understood, I think, I'm almost sure, in any case she went along with it, at least for a while, rocking there with me, on her couch, her frame remarkably thin, even bony, really, certainly fragile, for what seemed like several minutes, although it was probably more like seconds, and finally I looked at my watch and like in a bad movie said I had to be going, had to be getting home, and I did, have to be going, getting home, across town, and having thanked her, her having thanked me, in a way that said this was wonderful, really wonderful, a small cusp of miracle, although it went without saying no matter what we ever thought of doing again it could never be this, not in this life, and so I went across town, arriving near midnight, the sky aglow with the lights from the nuclear plant, home, where I sat in the chair near our bed and, well, simply stared at my wife sleeping, and I won't say that love for her flooded me, exactly, I won't be that pedestrian, I won't say that all at once I fell deeply in love with her all over again, no, that wasn't it, but I want to say I felt, what ... good, really, yes, I felt like I could sit still for hours and just observe her, which allowed a kind of peace to expand inside of me as if something rich among my lungs had just ruptured and begun to leak, and I must have glided along the glassy edge of sleep then, that dark rich sleep where there are no dreams whatsoever, no awareness, because ... because then ... because then I was suddenly hearing my daughter's screams, and I was rising, and the bed beside me was already empty.

THE LIGHT-HAIRED CHILD IN HIS ARMS
I want to go *back*, daddy! I want to go *back*!

THE FIGURE WHOSE LEFT ARM IS RAISED
This last figure, of course, represents you. It represents the intrigue you've experienced for years in the presence of Max Ernst's assemblage. It represents your faithful visits to the Museum of Modern Art, once every week (except those two months your mother was ill), climbing the wide gray staircase in that vast grayness smelling of dust and diesel. Represents how

you stood before the piece, devoted to the act of wondering. Can one compose a story behind its story? Represents how you slowly developed your own assemblage, smaller, more monochromatic, based on a conflation of this one and your dreams of falling, all the while trying (and failing) to find the connection among its mysterious and complex images, unaware that tomorrow the curatorial staff will discover the shadowy figure was not, in art historical fact, a shadowy figure at all, but a mistake, a blemish on the canvas, and will, meticulously and with great fanfare in the local media, wipe it off.

FROM

Scherzi, I Believe

(1994)

Family

ZACH HAD BEEN SPLITTING WOOD most of the morning down by the shed when he first sniffed the familiar scent of his father who had died five years before in a mining accident. It was early spring and pale green buds fuzzed the birches along Amos Ridge and the ground was soggy and almost black with runoff. Zach straightened and let the axe swing down by his side. He sniffed the air again like a cat suddenly aware of chicken livers on the kitchen counter. The intimate aroma was hard to pin down. Some honey was in it. Some salt. Cinnamon was there. Maybe some sourdough and pine needles. He hadn't smelled anything like it for half a decade but recognized it right away, down behind his stomach. It didn't frighten him and it didn't gladden him. It was more interest he felt.

He turned and squinted a little into the intense sunshine fanning through the branches around him and saw his father standing with his hands in his pockets in a misty golden nimbus near a wild dogwood. He looked just as he had on the day he left the cabin for the last time, wearing overalls and olive-green rubber tie-up boots and a stained undershirt and yesterday's beard. They stood there eyeing each other several heartbeats. Then Zach nodded in a gesture of acknowledgement and his father's ghost nodded back and Zach turned and picked up his axe and picked up a foot-and-a-half pine log and set it upright on the stump before him and started splitting once more because there was still a good part of an hour left until lunchtime.

Strip mining had peaked outside of Frenchburg, Kentucky, in the late sixties and early seventies and then began falling off. Houses went up for sale. Ken's Market, one of the two grocery stores in town, shut down. The lone car dealership burned to the ground one night and nobody seemed to have enough money to clean up the charred remains. But Zach's father didn't have much else he felt comfortable doing so he decided to stick with mining as long as mining would stick with him. The company had brought in a mechanical monster called Little Egypt to make the job of digging more cost-efficient. Little Egypt was a machine the size of a small hotel. It was several stories tall and several stories wide and was covered with gears the size of most men. Little Egypt looked more like something people would use on Mars for exploration than it did something people would use in Meniffee County for mining. Its sole purpose was to dig itself into the earth, slowly, cumbersomely, relentlessly, twenty-four hours a day, seven days a week, three-hundred and sixty-five days a year, processing coal as it went, eating, gnawing, wheezing and clanking with a deafening sound. Zach's father, who was fifty-seven at the time, was part of the team of men responsible for keeping the huge gears clear of crushed stone and grit and for keeping them oiled and running smoothly. One day in late summer during his lunch break Zach's father sampled a swig too much shine a buddy of his had offered and tripped as he was shinnying among the intricate workings of the behemoth.

At noon Zach's wife, Amelia, called him for lunch. She had made bean soup and black bread and apple cobbler. He washed his hands at the spigot outside and walked around his dark blue Ford pickup and went in and sat at the table near the stove and began to eat. Amelia told him how she was going into town to pick up some things and Zach told her how he was going to start patching the aluminum roof on the shed that had blown off during a big storm last November. Amelia told Zach how she had phoned Madge at the next farm over and how Madge and Opal's dog had been bitten by the first copperhead of the season and how the dog's snout had grown a lump that made it appear as if it were raising a plum under the flesh. As Zach listened he became aware of his father standing by the refrigerator, hands in the pockets of his overalls, watching the couple talk and eat. He wasn't smiling and wasn't frowning but his eyes seemed a little more yellowish than usual and they seemed sad. He didn't speak and didn't move. He just looked on as Zach raised a forkful of apple cobbler to his mouth and then washed it down with a gulp of water. Amelia noticed Zach was staring hard and long at the refrigerator and turned to see what he was looking at.

Your father's here, she said.

Yep, said Zach, cutting himself another bite of cobbler. I reckon he is.

And that's how it started: Zach's father just appeared one beautiful spring day in a misty golden nimbus and Zach and Amelia acknowledged his appearance and then they didn't say a whole bunch else about it. After all, they had a lot of other things to think about. The field down the road needed plowing and planting. The shed needed mending. The winter wood needed stacking. And if they knew anything about Zach's father they knew he could take care of himself.

Zach had the impression his father had come to tell him something he didn't already know. Maybe some secret about life fathers come back to tell their sons because it's so considerable. But Zach's father never spoke. In fact he never made any sort of sound, not even when he walked across the wooden kitchen floor in his olive-green rubber tie-up boots. Zach waited two weeks, thinking his father might be trying to find the right words in which to stick his wisdom. And when Zach figured maybe his father could use some coaxing, he prompted him one rainy night by asking: So what do you have to say for yourself?

His father had nothing to say for himself. His facial expression didn't change. His eyes continued to look more yellowish than usual and sad and they focused on Zach's moving lips and then on Zach's blue eyes and it occurred to Zach that the problem was his father couldn't hear a word he was saying. There must have been some kind of interference between this world and the next. So he got a slip of paper and pencil and came back and wrote down his question and tried to give it to his father but the paper passed through his father's extended hand as though it were no more than colored air and fluttered to the floor.

When Zach told his wife, she said she was convinced his father had come back to visit them because death was such a lonely place.

It ain't, Zach said. Lots of people are dead. He has plenty of company where he's at.

That's what you know, Zach Ingram, Amelia said.

She let Zach's father accompany her from room to room and when she went outside to hang clothes and clean the outhouse. He followed her at a respectful distance and took what seemed an exquisite interest in the chores of daily life: baking muffins, boiling pot roast, frying potatoes, scrubbing the skillet, folding down the quilt on the bed, hanging the winter coats in the back of the closet until next fall. She set a place for him at dinner and even put scraps on his plate although he couldn't sit without falling through the chair and when he bent down and tried to pick up a crumb with his tongue the crumb passed right through his jaw. She lit a candle for him every evening and put it on the kitchen table and bought a newspaper for him to read every Sunday when she headed to church even though she knew he wouldn't be able to hold it. Every night he stood in their bedroom door when they were ready to go to sleep until they said good night to him and turned off the lights and then he would wander into the living room and stand by the window and wait for the first gray glow of dawn. Sometimes Zach would come upon him standing at the end of Amos Ridge on Whippoorwill Point amid wild blueberry bushes and sassafras shrubs, looking out over the limestone cliffs and pines and cedars below, or kneeling by the thousands of large amazing jelly-bubble frog-egg sacks in puddles in the ruts along the dirt road leading up to the cabin.

They had no idea how good his presence made them feel until one morning in July Amelia went into the kitchen at six o'clock to grind some coffee and discovered he was gone. She thought he must be in the living room at the window watching the sun roll up behind the trees but when she checked no one was there. She stuck her head into all the closets and went outside and searched the shed and the outhouse and the area around the woodpile. She woke Zach and told him what had happened and he dressed and headed down to Whippoorwill Point and when he didn't find him there walked all the way to Madge and Opal's farm before understanding he had lost his father a second time. He told Amelia what he hadn't discovered and sat down in a fold-up chair on the porch and didn't get up for three weeks.

He sat with his left ankle on his right knee and his hands in his lap and looked out over the ridge. The hot hazy sky purpled at twilight. Stars glittered on. And after a while he put his chin on his chest and fell asleep. In the morning he didn't eat breakfast and in the afternoon he didn't eat lunch and in the evening he didn't eat dinner. Gradually he became as quiet as his father had been. Amelia pointed out he was getting thinner and more pathetic every day and when he didn't respond she began to eat his meals in addition to her own. First it was simply a way not to let the food go to waste. Then it was a way to express her own grief. She gained five pounds the first week, eight pounds the second.

Late in August, as Zach watched the burning ball of the sun dip behind the tree line, he noticed two figures walking up the road toward him. Through half-closed eyes he took them to be Madge and Opal dropping by for a visit. But the closer the couple came the easier it was to tell they couldn't be Madge and Opal: the man was too old, the woman too short. Zach squinted and then he cocked his head to one side and then he shut one eye and then it struck him he was looking at his parents, both his parents, walking arm in arm up the road as they often did after dinner. His father was still wearing the same clothes he had on the day he fell into Little Egypt. His mother was wearing the nightshirt she wore the day she said living without her husband was a stupid foolish thing and crawled into her bed and turned her face to the wall. The couple mounted the porch and walked by Zach and he rose and followed them and saw them halt in the bedroom door, watching Amelia—now chubby, soft, round, and wide-eyed—watch them back from bed.

Zach's parents were extremely considerate. They always stood in corners, out of the way, arm in arm, or, at night, by the window in the living room from which they could see dawn graying into existence. They never asked for anything, offered advice, or nagged. They took obvious delight in the wood grain rippling through the kitchen table; the black-and-white patterns on the wings of the willet that appeared on the roof of the shed one cold autumn afternoon; the yellow-green tobacco leaves ready for harvest in the field down the road. Sometimes at dusk they craned their necks and closed their eyes and sniffed at the cool evening air filled with wet grass, endive, and leafy mulch. Sometimes they bent over a tall curl of wild grass and studied the shiny blue body of the dragonfly arched just above it.

Zach and Amelia barely noticed when his mother disappeared for two nights, returning with cousin Virgil, who had died at thirty when his sleek black Toyota pickup skidded off route 641 one rainy night in 1984 and smashed into a tree at eighty miles per hour. Or when Zach's father disappeared for nearly twenty-four hours, showing up cradling a baby in his arms, the Armstid's little girl, who had died last year when she was two weeks old because she had been born with some of her insides backward. Amelia was startled to see her uncle Farrell, who'd been killed in 1968 during the Tet Offensive, and her aunt Helen, who'd taken her own life in 1963 when she caught her husband Tom fooling around with that cheap blond Bobbie Ann Stills. Zach tried to shake hands with his nephew Billy, whose spine had snapped during an accident on his Honda ATV in 1993, and he tried to hug his mother's friend, Mildred, who'd been bitten by a rattler while picking raspberries in 1956 on Madge and Opal's farm. Zeb, whose tractor engine fell on him just last year while he was trying to tighten a bolt under it, showed up after all the leaves had dropped off the trees on Amos Ridge, and Abel, who choked on a chicken bone while watching the 1979 World's Series Game, appeared as the skies turned the color of a field mouse's neck and the first light snow began to fall.

House sure is getting mighty cramped, Zach said when he stayed in on Thanksgiving to watch the Macy's parade on TV.

Family's family, Amelia said.

Zach knew she was right and so he didn't say anything else. He felt good. He felt a system of harmonies forming around him and had an abrupt sense of being somewhere. Only he had to confess it was hard to see the TV set, what with little Dinamarie playing tag with Hazel and Gladys and Grace and Gary Bob in front of it and Angie smooching with George at the kitchen table and Susie and Flinn bopping each other over the heads because Flinn had decided to appropriate Susie's favorite rhinestone pinkie ring which he wouldn't give back and Uncle Gus was trying unsuccessfully to clean his .20-gauge shotgun on the living room floor.

Sleeping was difficult too because the children wanted to be in bed between Zach and Amelia and many of the adults felt the need to stretch out nearby on the floor. Zach couldn't turn over or get up to visit the outhouse and he could never show his affection for Amelia who had never stopped eating two portions of each meal every day and was now the size of a large flaccid dolphin. Little Ainsley and Harlan and Jake and Remus wanted to help with all the chores but continually got under foot. Amelia fared no better in the kitchen where her mother-in-law and aunts supervised all her cooking, which she now performed nearly fourteen hours a day. Although no one except Zach and her could eat, Amelia felt it only right to make enough for everyone. Sometimes at three in the morning she would rise and begin breakfast and sometimes after midnight she would still be cleaning dishes. Over the following weeks she turned big as a black bear whose stubby arms could no longer touch its sides. She turned big as a small manatee that plowed through the cabin, moving ponderously yet carefully because she had lost sensation in her extremities and could no longer feel whether or not she might be bumping into things or people. Her neck went away and she forgot what it was like to bend from the waist and she only vaguely remembered what her once beautiful red-painted toenails had looked like.

By February the food supply had run down and Zach felt more tired than ever before and Amelia could no longer walk, no longer even fit through the bedroom door. Zach arranged pillows and blankets for her to lie in on the living room floor and began feeding her through a funnel because she could no longer lift her hands. The flesh of her face tugged at her tiny miraculous brown eyes and made her look a little Japanese. Fat from her arms and legs puddled near her on the rug. It appeared as if she were melting. The ghosts grew fascinated by how she lay there gazing up at the ceiling, unable to speak just as they were unable to speak, partake of the world just as they were unable to partake. They seemed to understand Amelia was eating for all of them now, that her metabolism was digesting for the whole family. The adults kneeled around her. The children frolicked on her body as though it were an astonishingly soft playground. They burrowed under her breasts and slid down the smoothness of her thighs and curled by her massive head to nap.

Every day more relatives appeared: Samuella who had fallen down a well when she was three; Rachel who had cooked up some bad mushrooms when she was twenty-seven. More relatives than Zach could count, more than he could squeeze into the space of his imagination. They spilled out onto the porch and into the shed and by the middle of March they were sleeping in the woods all the way down to Whippoorwill Point and Zach couldn't go anywhere without stumbling upon them, surprised by their eyes staring back at him from around a corner or under a bush or behind a birch. He gave up on all his chores except feeding Amelia. He gave up all food except Amelia's food. The hot weather settled in and he realized he should have planted months ago. The cool weather replaced it and he realized he had nothing more for Amelia to eat and nothing more to grow next year and no more firewood for next fall and winter.

As the September sky blanched, Zach walked down to Madge and Opal's and borrowed some tools and supplies and began to construct a mobile pulley near his dark blue Ford pickup. The gizmo looked like an eight-foot-tall oil well. When it was done Zach removed the skeletal braces and rolled the contraption over to the sliding doors that led off the living room. He padded the sturdy wooden base with pillows and blankets and then went to the shed and got his snow shovel. He returned to the living room and gingerly navigated among the ghosts until he reached Amelia sprawled in the middle of the floor. He shoved his shovel under a lump of fat he took to be her flank and heaved. Haltingly he began to roll his gigantic doughy wife across the floor. She could not move herself and she could not speak but each time she found herself on her back she looked up at Zach with her exquisite brown eyes. Zach avoided her gaze and put his back into the work. He rolled her through the sliding doors and rolled her onto the porch and, having removed the banisters there, he rolled her over the edge and onto the padded mobile pulley that groaned and wheezed and shook under her enormous weight. Then he struggled and pushed and heaved the mobile pulley around toward the front of the cabin.

Half an hour later Amelia flooded the back of his pickup. Her rubbery arms and squelchy legs draped over the sides. She stared up at the trees above her. Zach climbed into the cab and turned on the engine and eased down the peddle. The shock absorbers creaked and swayed. The pickup lurched and commenced crawling down the dirt road. When it tapped the first bump the metal belly scraped sand and gravel. But Zach didn't pay any attention. He already felt his heart expanding. He blinked and smiled and looked up into the rearview mirror. All the dead people had collected outside the cabin behind him. They were watching the pickup creep down the driveway, winding its way toward Madge and Opal's and beyond. Zach saw them all raising their hands and waving goodbye. And, as he turned the corner, he caught a glimpse of them begin to follow.

Watch and Ward

I SIT IN MY BACKYARD PREPARING notes for a survey course I'm teaching on American literature from 1865 to the present. It is ten in the morning. Tuesday. My class is at two. Today I'll talk about the tension between the idea of the frontier and the idea of the settlement pervading American consciousness, and other clichés. Our text will be *Huck Finn*. About now I would normally pump my wife, Adrienne, for possible approaches. But I can't do that since she is still off somewhere with our son.

It is early October. I am drinking a scotch. Chivas. Yellow leaves infected with brown crinkle in the maples. Chilly funnels of breeze churn through the yard, miniature tornadoes, while I sip and jot. The geraniums in the flowerbed lining our garage have lost all their bright red heads, and the ivy spreading up the wall has tinged cinnamon. The sun is intense on my face and between windscuds it almost feels too warm in my sweater. It is that kind of autumn day filled with desire, where over at the dorms teens are ditching classes to saucer Frisbees through the air.

Two books meet in *Huck Finn,* I write. The text of the raft is romance, the universe of expansion and exploration. The text of the shore is realism, the universe of limitations and quarantine.

I raise my head, nibble my pencil, wonder where my wife is. Adrienne said there was no way I was getting rid of her after all this but there was also no way she could stand to look at my face for a while either. She has green eyes and wears a magical suntan year round. Unfortunately in her womb my genes conspired against her, and our son, whom I call behind his back, depending on my mood and his, St. Thomas or Doubting

Thomas, came out too short for his seven years, with a head too large for his forty-nine inches. Adrienne and I both fell in love with Idea of Comedy 247 and with each other as graduate students at the University of Wisconsin when people still threw tear gas in the morning and struck in the afternoon, and we happily bounced around the country for six years after we were married, looking for joint jobs. Thirteen months into this hopping, Thomas yammered along, never believing a thing dad said, and never being reprimanded even for the most outrageous offenses by mom, who was born peevish and who, I am sure, shall someday die that way.

What I really adore about the positions we finally landed weren't the positions we finally landed. What I really adored was the house we found nestled in a Moscow, Idaho, neighborhood with winding streets and lush trees and names like Homestead Place and Kamiaken Street and Mountainview Road where at night, as in my midwestern childhood, you can always hear a duodecaphonic symphony of crickets playing, and children tagging, and samoyeds yelping, and poodles yapping. The house is fifty-four years old and looks like an English cottage with weeping brick and brown trim and possesses, out back, a garage that has been made into a studio for Adrienne. Out front stands the most spectacular towering maple you are ever likely to see.

All June we spent repainting, patting in new carpet, buying secondhand bookcases, one couch, three living room chairs. All July we spent working outside, mowing, pruning, chopping, clipping, sweeping, planting marigolds and, of course, those bright red geraniums. Even Trooper Thomas pitched in. You can imagine the labor that went into something like that. And you can imagine how proud we were when we were finished, a dignified trio on the front lawn one afternoon surveying their estate, fifty-five feet across, one hundred and forty-eight feet deep.

You can also imagine how achingly surprised I was when Chief Eagle-Eye Thomas pointed to our next-door neighbors' lawn and said: Look, daddy, all their grass is dying.

It's supposed to look like that, I lied.

Go eat your lunch, Adrienne said, I think to Thomas.

I'm not hungry and it is *not* supposed to look like that, he said. And it makes *our* lawn look tacky.

Where did you learn a word like that—*tacky*? I asked, deflecting.

It looks like a desert, he answered.

Somehow when you're looking at houses to buy you miss so much. With ours we had overlooked the fact that the gas line feeding our fireplace had been detached, an evil omen by any standard. We had overlooked a biomorphic grease stain on the carpet under the kitchen table. And now it occurred to me we had overlooked the evidence suggesting the Gerstles were intent on letting their lawn die. All the other houses on the block had avocado green ones trimmed like baby golf courses. But when I looked this time, I didn't see any of them. What I saw was an oatmeal-colored wasteland next door. I patted my son on the head, too hard I'm afraid, and told him to do what his mother said. I went in to lunch and chomped away as though hopes and aspirations are things that parch every day.

That night as Adrienne turned off the light and the house went quiet and all you could faintly hear was the sparse traffic on the Troy Highway several blocks away, the image of that lawn began roaming around inside my head like a cat searching for shelter during a heavy rain. By four I was up, in my robe, downstairs, crossing my driveway, our garden hose and sprinkler dragging behind me. Noiselessly I set things up. And by the time the garbage truck tortoised up the street at five thirty, I was crossing my driveway in the opposite direction, our garden hose and sprinkler dragging behind me. I waved. The sanitation men waved. We both intuited we were in the midst of something important. By the time I met them again two weeks later, the Gerstles' lawn was coming to life.

If it had only been for that, of course, Adrienne would still be here with me to share my second scotch. But as I was crossing my driveway that morning I happened to glance up at the sun hanging like a glaring hole in the sky and stopped. Something else I had missed: the Gerstles' gutters were stuffed with corruption. Leaves. Dams of twigs. Wads of black ooze. I trotted up to our bedroom which looks down on their roof and stood amazed. Slimy puddles glistened in the morning light. A fungus-ridden branch cocked in a corner. Charcoal-colored acorns specked the shingles.

I woke Adrienne and asked her to accompany me. Bleary-eyed, baffled, she shuffled to the window and squinted out.

Fine, she said. They're pigs. Now go back to bed.

At breakfast I reminded her of what she'd seen.

She looked up from her grapefruit and said: Don't you have more pressing problems to worry about than this?

Like what?

Clear-cutting. Salmon netting. The spotted goddamn owl.

Apples and pears, I pointed out.

It's the Gerstles' business, she said.

That afternoon as I was writing up in my study I saw Mr. Gerstle, a young pink pudgy man, walking out his front door toward his car. I sprinted downstairs and intercepted him.

I guess I should introduce myself, I said. Your new neighbor, James Swenson. Jim.

I grinned, stuck out my hand.

Colin Gerstle, he said. Where you from?

I told him.

My wife and I've camped in the Penokees a couple times. Nice country.

Ah, I said, a camper.

Toxicologist, actually. You?

I teach at the University. English.

Oops! he said, lifting fist to face. Better watch my grammar, eh?

Nice lawn you have there, I said.

Gerstle looked around him, puzzled.

Yeah, he said. I guess.

What's the secret?

Nothing. We don't do a thing to it. Must be in the seed or something. Listen, I gotta run. He turned toward his car, a humdrum Honda. Real nice meeting you, he said. I'm sure we'll be seeing more of each other.

Well, I said, I hope I don't seem like I'm prying or anything, but I couldn't help noticing out our bedroom window that you've got a little problem with your gutters.

Gutters?

I pointed.

They're pretty clogged. Looks like a good cleaning's in order.

Yeah, right, he said. Guess the landlord'll get around to it eventually.
Landlord?

Stealing a glance at his watch, he said: Gosh, like I says, I gotta run. Thanks again though. Nice to meet you.

He disappeared into his car. The door thumped shut, the engine revved, and he was backing out of his driveway. I sprinted upstairs and began logging in hours. Within a few days I had a pretty good idea when the Gerstles were home and when they were out. So the next Wednesday I waited for Adrienne to leave for her midweek Pilates class, hauled our ladder from the garage, and got to work. I was just putting it back when Gerstle drove up again. As I strolled past him I nodded skyward.

Looks like your landlord's been by.

How about that, he said.

When Adrienne, Thomas, and I went on our daily after-dinner walk, a silent celebration on my part, we noticed the pink flamingos. Eight of them. On the front yard of the third house up the block from us, a lovely cedar-sided cottage. Eight pink plastic flamingos in various positions. Some strutted. Some paused in meditation. Some pointed north by an obese forsythia bush.

Oh God, Adrienne said.

Well, Jesus, I said.

It looks like grandma's house, Thomas said.

Stop laughing, I told Adrienne. And to Thomas: Grandma has *one,* not *eight,* flamingos. And hers are cement, not plastic. And don't laugh at your grandmother.

Plastic's not biodegradable, he said.

Where do you *learn* words like that? Plastic, Thomas, is *cheap.* No one has pink plastic flamingos on their front yard unless it's some kind of joke.

These people do, daddy.

I stared at him a moment, thinking.

I bet they'll be gone by morning, I said.

After I turned on the sprinkler at the Gerstles next sunrise, I walked up the avenue with my garden shears and clipped the bawdy birds off at the backwards knees. When we took our next after-dinner stroll, all the corpses had vanished.

Daddy, I proclaimed, is not as stupid as he looks.

What? shouted Thomas.

He couldn't hear me because of the chain saw whirring at the house across the street. A gray man in his sixties was standing in his driveway, jellybelly over belt, oily blue exhaust eating him, blissfully gnashing away at one dreamy tree after another.

They were maples, mostly. Some twenty feet tall. He was working on the fourth one when I reached him. He told me he was cutting down a couple trees on his property so it could get some more sun. I mentioned the soaring incidents of skin cancer in the United States, pointed out the name of the street on which we were living was Maple Avenue and that if he continued along his present course of action it might as well be called Oak or Birch. He laughed at me and behind me Thomas chimed in. My son always loved to see things come down.

Two nights later I hopped fences and dodged dogs, under my arm a box full of saplings I'd bought earlier in the day. Carefully I knelt in the dusty morning light and planted more than thirty of them. When I passed that afternoon they were still up.

Not long after that I fixed a flat on the Williams' red '67 Mustang after they left it squatting in their driveway like that for five days. I swept the Wrobels' sidewalk. I picked the over-ripe beans in the Garvins' garden and, when they were away on vacation, washed the McCafferys' bird-bespattered picture window. I knocked the dents out of the Rikkis' trash cans and sprinkled some grass seed on the bare patches on the Sheldons' front lawn. I slept very little, maybe four hours a night, since most of my work came when the suburbs snored. I spent over six-hundred dollars on my projects, but slowly, very slowly, our neighborhood's rough edges disappeared. It turned cleaner, trimmer, more aesthetically stylish than I could have imagined.

My literature course began about then and I found myself putting a particularly large emphasis on the development of the police force in America. Often I digressed, listening to myself explain how the English colonists brought over what they called the watch-and-ward system of security. Back then the men who stood guard did so in their own neighborhoods and without pay. It worked beautifully because everyone had a stake in the job. They had a reason to listen, look, protect. But when Texas instituted the first state police system in 1835 and Boston set up the first paid police force three years later, things started going downhill and they've been going down hill ever since, as far as I'm concerned, because a rift opened between those who watched and those who were watched.

My own would have succeeded just fine had I not become faintly overzealous and set the Cues' powder-blue speedboat on fire. One day they dragged it up and parked it on their front yard, took the canvas cover off it, and just left it there. At first I thought Mr. Cue was tinkering on it for the afternoon. Only it was still perched on the lawn next morning. Then I tried to convince myself he'd put it on sale and it would be gone in a day or two. He didn't tinker on it, though, and it didn't go anywhere. It roosted there, phallic and loathsome, and when I phoned Mr. Cue and held a handkerchief over the mouthpiece and disguised my voice and asked him what the hell he was doing destroying the charm of our community, he asked me if I liked water-skiing.

What the hell does that have to do with anything? I asked.

If you've never water-skied, he said, you will never in a million years understand the beauty of a boat.

That night I lugged over a gallon of gas and a red pack of matches and torched it. Or almost torched it. The gas was poured, the acrid scent in the gray air, the match in my hand, the pale blue-orange flame wobbling on the end of the thin white stick. And then the patrol car swung around the corner.

I bolted. They chased. A siren shrilled behind me. And I skidded and tumbled on the Gerstles' wet grass I'd been watering. Next thing I knew a frail young man, no more than twenty-five, was holding a gun to the back of my head.

Suh-suh-suh stop, he stammered.

Don't shuh-shuh-shuh shoot, I answered in his language.

The white sunball angles over my maples, falls like fine electricity on my face. I pour my third golden scotch and sip. It is almost eleven now.

Nothing I've done has hurt anyone. I want to make that clear. Adrienne told me she agreed before she packed her bags and packed Troubled Thomas and left me for a while. Mr. Cue didn't press charges, bless his speedboat. Neither did the Maple Man, the Flamingo Kid, or the others. That said, no one speaks to me either. No one pays me any attention. No one waves, bleeps as they pass by. All of which sends a tiny squirrel of pain skedaddling through my chest, but you know how these things are. They take time. People tell me that every afternoon on the talk shows I've taken to watching. Someday I will catch up on the classes I've lost telling about early American police forces. Someday Adrienne will come back to me. Someday Thomas will doubt again, this time with good reason. And someday every person on Maple Avenue will nod at me as they walk or drive past, as though they are doing me a favor, and on that day I shall become just like everyone else, just another guy next door, and on that day I shall be able to begin taking care of them all once more.

Moving

MIA AND MURPHY WERE THE KIND of people who provoked mild envy on the part of their friends. They had been happily married nine years. They had bought and renovated a charming sixty-year-old house in a densely foliaged neighborhood in North Seattle. They went to films regularly. Their tastes were eclectic, neither too experimental nor too conventional. They enjoyed the Marx Brothers, Werner Herzog, and *Grey's Anatomy*. They played squash three times a week, owned a large-screen TV and a baby blue Volvo. Mia sculpted but didn't feel she was ready yet to go professional. She created smooth curved pieces with many holes in them out of inexpensive stone. Murphy had a satisfactory job at the university teaching twentieth-century British literature to students who had never been on a plane, never left the country, never been out of the state, and who returned to their homes in various suburbs every weekend having forgotten what Murphy had taught them. Mia and Murphy traveled to conferences in Arizona, Florida, and Hawaii, but never attended the lectures. Instead, they rented cars and toured their new circumstances. They entertained informally once a week.

Mia and Murphy hoped someday a more prestigious seat of learning would approach him so they could move to an exciting metropolis. Los Angeles, perhaps. New York. They hoped someday to have children, a boy and a girl.

The phone call that changed their plans arrived one bright May afternoon. Murphy was trimming the hedge in the front yard. The sky was the color of wisteria and the breeze carried the fragrance of last autumn's leaves, mulch, and sunlight. Murphy was wearing tattered jean cutoffs and a white t-shirt. His hands were stinging and vibrating in a pleasant way. He wasn't thinking about anything in particular, just the even hedge before him, the clatter and buzz in his head, when Mia appeared by his side and announced that the chair of Murphy's department, Richard Wescott, was on the phone. Richard was sixty-one, had in the course of his career written three articles on the prosody of an anonymous medieval poem, and wore intensely worried blue eyes. During departmental meetings he picked at his knuckles. He and Murphy had always been on friendly terms, although after bumping into Richard in the halls Murphy was usually left with the impression Richard only sporadically remembered his name.

I have some bad news for you, Richard announced.

Bad news? Murphy said, looking out the window at Mia who was still standing in the backyard, hands on hips, examining Murphy's work. Her frizzy hair reached halfway down her back. It was the color of sandpaper. The cusps of her buttocks revealed themselves slightly beneath the ragged hem of her jean cutoffs.

Richard's bad news came as no surprise to Murphy. During his five years at the university, Murphy had written four articles (one more, he felt it important to emphasize to himself, than Richard) on the prosody of Yeats' early poetry. These articles had been published in respectable journals that no one in the profession read unless they themselves were working on an article in which they needed to demonstrate their command of or disdain for past scholarship.

Looking out the window, Murphy saw these natural phenomena: a diamond-strung cobweb glinting between branches; the black crested crown, orange bill, and forked tail of a tern as it paused momentarily on the fence and then darted away; the acorn-gray of a chipmunk scuttling through uncut grass, belly low to the ground; and Mia standing by bushes filled with yellow flowers, hands on hips, face now turned toward Murphy, eyes wide and questioning, mouth expanding silently around one word: *What?*

Murphy went into his office the next day and signed what is called a terminal contract. The essence of a terminal contract is that the person who signs it has one year to find a new position, after which he will be let go. Their friends immediately began to look at Mia and Murphy with the sympathetic look they usually reserved for children born without fingers or noses. They held dinners in Mia and Murphy's honor and told the couple how much they would miss them and how Mia and Murphy had to keep in touch and how given the current state of disrepair at the university Mia and Murphy had probably dodged a bullet. They agreed with each other it was a shame Murphy had decided not to publish more during his five years in the department but said they were sure with his talent and excellent credentials he would have no difficulty in securing a new position somewhere else. Everything, they assured themselves, would work out in the end.

When Murphy finished grading his final exams in mid-May he did not begin looking for another job. Mia and he climbed into their baby blue Volvo and drove into the mountains and camped for two weeks. They hiked, fished, swam naked in ice-cold lakes. They visited Mia's father in Des Moines and Murphy's mother in Detroit. They did not return home until July and remained only forty-eight hours before they climbed back into their baby blue Volvo and drove to the Southwest to visit friends they hadn't seen since their wedding. They had such a good time Murphy lost track of what day it was and somehow didn't make it back to the university until the second week of classes that fall.

Their friends said this was perfectly understandable. Mia and Murphy needed time to cut loose … and yet, these friends couldn't help adding, now it was time for Murphy to buckle down and start his job search in earnest. If he played his cards right, he could have a new position by February. To everyone's surprise, though, Murphy didn't buckle down. He didn't start his job search in earnest.

The couple sold their baby blue Volvo instead. Their friends were dumbstruck. What was going on here? Before they could arrive at an answer—it was September—Mia and Murphy sold their TV as well. They stopped going to films, then stopped renting videos. When Richard Wescott sent around a form asking each faculty member to project travel expenses for the spring semester Murphy sent his back blank except for his name and social security number in the upper left and right corners, respectively. Mia and Murphy played squash two times a week, then one time a week, and then they ceased altogether. Mia continued sculpting until her supplies ran out in November, then packed up her smooth curved pieces with many holes in them and put them in the basement. Her friends told her she should try selling some but she told them she still wasn't ready to go professional. They asked her confidentially how Murphy's job search was progressing and Mia answered it was progressing pretty much the same as usual. They asked her confidentially if she had given any thought to part-time work and she answered: No. None at all. Why do you ask?

We love them dearly, their friends said when Murphy didn't show up at the annual professional convention to interview for jobs. Rumors circulated. Bob and Nancy Hutchinson said they heard Mia and Murphy were thinking about joining a commune in Oregon. Brenna Phelps over in classics said she thought she had heard they were going into some sort of business together, catering or some such thing, but she couldn't remember the details. Stuart Wilkins in linguistics said he had bumped into Mia and Murphy at a cocktail party several weeks ago at somebody's house and Murphy had told him he had accepted a job somewhere in Massachusetts at a college whose name began with a B, unless it was someone else Stuart Wilkins had bumped into. Ulrica Thornsen in German, who wanted nothing so much in life as to be pregnant, said she thought she had heard Mia was pregnant.

A For Sale sign appeared in Mia and Murphy's front lawn. Before the spring meeting of the Academic Organization and Structure Committee was to convene, Franny Gibson in psychology turned and asked Marvin Butler in English if he had seen Mia and Murphy lately. Come to think of it, Marvin Butler said, I haven't. Marvin asked Rufus Michelles in French and Rufus Michelles in French asked Seymour Kratzke in German and Seymour Kratzke in German asked Vito and Geraldine Pettit at the library and it turned out that no one had seen Mia and Murphy. A sense of communal befuddlement ensued. Denise Canetti in English was convinced Mia and Murphy had already moved, she believed to New Jersey (she had parents in New Jersey). Dan and Belinda Roberts in economics were convinced Mia and Murphy hadn't already moved but neither could account for why no one answered Mia and Murphy's phone or doorbell. They exchanged glances and shook their heads solemnly as they might have at the funeral of a seventeen-year-old girl tragically mowed down in the prime of her life by a drunk driver.

Mia and Murphy's names slowly dropped out of conversation. Nothing deliberate or malicious motivated this. They just ceased to come up. There were, after all, more immediate problems to discuss. Denise Canetti's mother died. Brenna Phelps was having an affair with that lovely blond graduate student of hers. And the president of the university was forced by the governor to cut the budget for the third year in a row which meant there would be no raises again. But once at a dinner party given for Lucian Ross, the new assistant professor of twentieth-century British literature, Lucian, tipsy on wine, offhandedly said to Richard Wescott during a conversational lull: So tell me about Murphy. What sort of guy was he? Richard looked at Lucian for a moment with his intensely worried blue eyes. Then he looked at his wife, Ernestine, who looked back at him blankly. Then he looked at Lucian and said: Who?

Mia, who balanced their checkbooks, announced one May evening in an unexceptional voice they had run out of money. Murphy put down the magazine he had been reading and phoned the local newspaper. He placed an ad for all their furniture, cash only. Then Mia and Murphy slipped on their baby blue windbreakers, opened the front door, and went out for a walk.

They strolled hand-in-hand through the densely foliaged neighborhood, looking in lighted windows and discussing the fine weather. An exquisite full moon, big as a tractor tire, white as Caribbean sand, touched the treetops. Moist grass and soil sweetened the air. Cats moved low to the earth, staying close to bushes and stone walls. Mia and Murphy wandered down one street and up another. They curved through winding lanes, ambled up small shady hills in silver light, rounded a number of corners until they found themselves among older and older homes, more and more complex networks of avenues. Some houses dated from the turn of the century. Some appeared to have been built in the 1860s and 1870s. Many were made of great gray slabs and some even had fat columns out front. Looking and talking, they strolled serpentine streets with names they no longer recognized, and soon found themselves standing on the sidewalk before a lovely ivy-covered limestone cottage nestled in a small lot of pines and huge intricate bushes. In the front yard cocked a For Sale sign.

The cottage was dark but if they squinted and employed their peripheral vision Mia and Murphy could tell there were no curtains in the windows, no car in the gravel driveway. They counted to three hundred to make sure no one was moving behind the glass that caught the moon. A breeze tinged with pine pulsed and died. Murphy let go of Mia's hand and went to the front door. Mia watched Murphy ring the bell, wait, ring again, glance up at the night sky, rock back and forth on the balls of his feet. He put his hands in his pockets and took them out. He glanced over his shoulder at Mia and smiled. He rang the doorbell once more, then in a fluid gesture hopped off the front porch, ducked behind a hedge that ran along the front of the house, and disappeared around the corner. Mia heard a gate squeak open and shut. She began to count but changed her mind and scratched her neck. A few minutes, and Murphy returned, signaling for her to follow.

The small backyard, all pines and pine needles, was protected by a six-foot-tall wooden-plank fence. Mia and Murphy went from window to window cupping their hands and peering inside. The rooms were empty, the walls eggshell white, the hardwood floors sheening in bright moonlight. A small fireplace with a red brick mantle hunched in the living room. The den contained sunken bookshelves. In the center of the kitchen ceiling was an old-fashioned wooden fan. There was only one bedroom on the first floor but it was clear from the placement of the windows that there had to be another room, maybe two, upstairs. Murphy got down on his hands and knees under the kitchen window and Mia carefully stepped onto his back. In this position it took her just under two minutes to jimmy the latch.

Inside the air was dead and smelled of paint and old clothes. The water, gas, and electricity had been shut off. The kitchen carried a milky pong. Mia said she liked the tub with lion's paws in the bathroom, the white-

and-black tiled floor. Murphy said he liked the loft upstairs, a wide high open space, wood-paneled, and the two skylights. Mia opened and closed closets in the bedrooms, drawers in the kitchen, discovered a dented aluminum flashlight on a shelf in the pantry. There were only two windows in the basement, both facing the backyard, and they were easy enough to cover with the opaque plastic paper used to line the kitchen cabinets. The sump pump smelled like mildew and algae, but that was fine.

The following night they unrolled their sleeping bags down there and set up their chemical toilet and the camping shower near the sump pump. They brought in plastic water jugs and food in small knapsacks. They slept soundly, Murphy dreaming of sitting erect in a chair while flying at incredibly fast speeds through the Grand Canyon, Mia of floating comfortably seventy feet below the surface of the Atlantic Ocean. Their days began to order themselves. They woke around five, packed their equipment and placed it in a corner so it appeared as though the previous owners had forgotten it, and went out. They wandered through the market downtown, Mia sketching sides of beef, rows of headless turkeys hanging by their feet, skinned rabbits. They browsed in bookstores, read to each other, talked with each other for hours and hours. Mia once again fell in love with Murphy's firm bottom. Murphy once again fell in love with Mia's large wonderful breasts. They explored each other's bodies every night, astounded to uncover phenomena they had never uncovered before: a single strand of raven hair on Murphy's blond head; a fine fuzz above Mia's thin upper lip; a fleck of gold at the lower curve of Murphy's green, green iris.

The cottage was shown frequently that summer yet no one ever made an offer. It was too small for most families and the economy was struggling. In October the rains came. A chilly fog, gray as a pigeon's neck, descended on the city. People turned melancholy and stayed in their houses, forgetting things. The realtor brought by fewer and fewer prospective buyers. Blue spiders the size of fists scrabbled from beneath the kitchen cabinets and darted at Mia's ankles as she stepped from the basement in the morning. Mia and Murphy spent nights in their clothes, sleeping bags zipped together, curled into question marks. One day every week Murphy ventured into nearby neighborhoods and cleared gutters for money with which he bought a small butane heater. Mia and Murphy ate turkey sandwiches on Thanksgiving, made love for long hours in exotic positions, dreamed of skiing down snowy mountains without skis. For Christmas, Mia gave Murphy a gold plastic decoder ring she received from a gumball machine. Murphy gave Mia a collection of colorful pencils and a new pad in which to sketch. The icy earth began to thaw in February and six-inch purple-white worms oozed onto the sidewalks to drown in warm puddles. Trees budded. Plants nudged through black soil. Murphy bought a radio in March and sat with Mia in the loft and turned it on. Mia and Murphy thought maybe they had missed some important event during the winter but as they listened to the news they realized they hadn't.

Mia punched Murphy in the arm. He was dreaming of mercurochrome-colored butterflies and mosquitoes the width of hummingbirds. He knew he would wake up three seconds before he woke up. Then he was sitting in the lotus position, alert. The back door banged above them again. Feet stomped through the kitchen. There were voices everywhere. Murphy felt the deep vibration of an engine in his chest. Mia was on her knees, rolling her sleeping bag into a tight bundle. Murphy began packing too. He turned off the butane heater and collected empty water jugs and plastic plates. The footsteps moved into the hall. Someone opened the basement door, closed it. Mia and Murphy worked quickly and precisely. The footsteps moved into the kitchen. Someone laughed and then someone else laughed. Someone turned on music and the cottage filled with rock'n'roll. Something heavy dragged across the living room floor. Mia finished, went to one of the windows that faced the back yard. She stood on tiptoes and rapidly peeled away the opaque paper used to line the kitchen cabinets. Murphy propped their equipment in a corner so it appeared as though the previous owner had forgotten it, joined Mia, got down on his hands and knees. Mia carefully stepped onto his back.

A moment later they were crawling through pine needles. It was a bright spring day. The air smelled of warm wet grass. They stood up in a clearing, wiped the moist soil off their knees and palms. The breeze carried the fragrance of last autumn's leaves, mulch, and sunlight. They didn't think about anything in particular. Mia looked at Murphy and Murphy looked at Mia and they grinned with a sense of accomplishment, then turned and walked around the side of the cottage, down the gravel driveway, past the orange and white U-Haul rumbling near the street, past the Sold sign cocked in the front yard.

Two men in white t-shirts and blue jeans brattled in back of the truck and trundled down its ramp balancing a chest-of-drawers between them. One had slick blond hair and wore Buddy Holly glasses. The other had slick black hair and a heart-shaped tattoo on his upper arm. They caught sight of Mia and Murphy and gave them friendly smiles and halted at the bottom of the ramp. Mia and Murphy halted and smiled too.

Hey, the one with slick blond hair said.

Hey, said Murphy said.

You folks live round here? asked the one with the heart-shaped tattoo on his upper arm.

We used to, Murphy said. We just moved. Great neighborhood. You're going to love it here.

They stood and looked at each other, smiling, having run out of things to say.

Yeah, well, the man with the heart-shaped tattoo on his arm said. He nodded at the chest-of-drawers.

Murphy smiled and stood aside to let them pass.

Nice meeting you, Mia called after them.

As the two men moved up the sidewalk another man and a woman came out the front door of the cottage. The man was very thin and had long orangish hair. The woman was trim and had short dark hair. They walked quickly by Mia and Murphy, and ascended the ramp leading to the back of the U-Haul. Mia and Murphy watched them for a few moments, waiting to see if they wanted to talk, too. But they didn't, so Mia and Murphy turned and began strolling up the winding street, paying attention.

Thirty Messages

1. THE ONE YOU WEREN'T WAITING FOR
Hi Gilby. I've seen the face of God.

2. LOVE STORY
Cardie, great rump a grand valentine when she stooped, sunflashed red-gold hair, ebony eyes, small raised imperfection on her left shoulder, lived in Sligo, worked in the pub just around the corner and over the cement bridge from Yeats's poorly marked museum house. Wade, mouth too tiny for his face, baby jaw seemingly transplanted in place of his own, nose too large and peppered with pores, upper torso like a cockroach's perched atop insectile legs, lived in Bozeman and worked in Martin's Dry Wall Office on Main Street. They never met.

3. TWO FEET
Near the end of his life, Wittgenstein wrote secret notes to himself. He wanted to wake himself up in the midst of his dreaming. Why do I not satisfy myself that I have two feet when I want to get up from the chair? he asked himself on paper. There is no why. I simply don't. This is how I act.

4. WHY IS THIS HOW I ACT?
Last night I was dreaming I was dreaming. I heard a rustling by the window in my bedroom and opened my eyes. A dwarf was trying to scrabble in. I rose and walked across the room and tried to push the dwarf back

out the window. His face was the face of a bat. He snapped at me with his tiny bat canines. The window was on the second floor. His wings when my left palm brushed them felt like wet rubber. My right hand was on his forehead. He tilted back his neck and nipped my palm. No blood came from the wound. Suddenly I woke from that dream into another, higher-order dream in which I heard a rustling by the window in my bedroom. I opened my eyes and guess what I saw trying to scrabble in?

5. ANGELS IN YOUR GARDEN

Okay okay okay. Picture this. Two angels walking through your garden at dawn. Fog suffused by peach sunlight. Flowers sweet as honey. Et cetera. The angels are arm-in-arm, faces white light, hands glowing, but they exist in another dimension. I assert they're there. Prove they're not. If you say you don't see them, I tell you they're invisible. If you say you don't hear them, I tell you they walk on air without breathing. Take a photograph of your garden with no angels in it. Produce a recording filled with the frequency of birds chirping, a distant plane hurtling, perhaps even your own embarrassed cough in the background, which proves only your own existence—and I'll ask: How do I know the photograph hasn't been retouched, the tape altered? How do I know you didn't miss the angels by a millisecond, a bissextile year? Go on. Take an x-ray. Set a trap. Hide with me behind a row of Queen Mother plums for one hour, a decade, waiting, listening, witnessing. But quick, Gilby: look behind you! They've been standing there the whole time. You can almost smell them, can't you?

6. MENINGITIS

Near the end of his life, Wilde lay in a shabby Parisian hotel room. He had zero money, zero friends, zero identity. He had registered under a false name so he would bring no more embarrassment to his family and could expire in peace. He awoke from a series of hallucinations, gazed around him, met the eyes of his doctor, the only other person in the room, and pronounced his last words.

Either that wallpaper goes, he said, or I do.

7. WHO IS INTERESTED IN YOU?

You may not be interested in absurdity, but absurdity is interested in you. From Barthelme. Old stuff.

8. NEUTRINOS IN YOUR GARDEN

And what about *them?* Particles emitted during the decay of neutrons and mesons? Two neutrinos spinning through your garden at dawn. Fog suffused by peach et cetera. You assert they're there. How can I prove they're not? I can't see them, I say, hear them. They exist, you say. Show me, I say. I can't, you say. Weigh them for me, I say. They don't possess mass, you say. Display their electrical magic, I say. They're electrically neutral, you say. Measure them, I say. They don't react with measuring apparatus, you say. *Dah!* I say, then how do you know they exist? For without them, you say, the universe would fly apart. But quick, quick, Gilby: look behind you! No. No. Forget it. But that fragrance sweet as honey. Smell it? That isn't the flowers.

9. WHO IS INTERESTED IN YOU?

We all are, Gilby. Why don't you return our messages? Your friends love you. We respect you as an individual. We know you're hiding from us. What have we done to you? What haven't we?

10. ONE HAND

Hello? Gilby? Hello? You there? Pick up. Pick up your phone. Pick up your phone. Pick up your phone, Gilby. Pick up your phone. Hello? Pick up your phone. Gilby?

11. WHAT'S MY LINE AGAIN?

So every person in the world who in some way touches my life has been paid to act his or her part. Disprove it. Go ahead. Try. Well, you say, just ask them. But whatever they say is part of the script to which I'm not privy. Sneak up on them when they're not looking, you say, hide in a closet, crawl under a bed, wait for them to speak when they don't think you're around. But that's simply part of the same script which says I'm hiding in the closet or under the bed, waiting for them to speak while pretending I'm not around. Ockham's razor, then. Principle of parsimony. Plurality is not to be assumed without necessity. But but but: that's my *point*. It's more parsimonious to assume everyone in the universe is working off a script I don't have access to than to assume every man, woman, and child is running willy-nilly through a multidimensional pluriverse, scriptless. So what now? You can hear the angels laughing, white light issuing from their mouths like frozen breath.

12. THEATER

Near the beginning of his career, Tom Stoppard sat sunk like a gremlin in the back row of the London theater watching *Roz and Guil's* opening night. On stage several characters spoke about being on stage. Death followed by eternity, Rosencrantz said, or perhaps Guildenstern, the worst of both worlds. Stoppard's friend beside him leaned over and whispered, what's this damn thing about?

It's about to make me rich, Stoppard answered.

13. THE ONE YOU WEREN'T WAITING FOR

Hi Gilby. My mistake. It wasn't God's face after all.

14. PAW

Late autumn afternoon and you're trailing through a web of black aspens. The terrain opens upon a pearl pond. You circle once, kneel down, touch your fingertips to its cold surface. After several minutes you stand and search for the path that will lead you on. As you are about to enter the woods again, something at shoulder level catches your eye. Hanging in a thorny bush nearby is the leg of a small animal. You guess raccoon. Four inches. Cocked at elbow. Silver charcoal fur. A tiny paw with precise digits, forefinger pointing skyward, sharp milky nails. Torn off cleanly at the shoulder, like a drumstick, fresh raw flesh and muscle and glistening joint. You look around for the rest of the carcass but can't locate it. There's no sign of struggle, trap, no fur on the ground for a hundred yards in any direction. The leaves at the base of the bush remain untouched. What sort of astonishment would you have seen had you broken through half an hour earlier?

15. TELEPHONE CALL TO NEW YORK

Does my telephone call to New York strengthen my conviction that the earth exists? Wittgenstein wondered.

16. BRAINS

It's simple coincidence that every person whose skull has been opened has had a brain in it. Go ahead. Prove me wrong. Open up the head of someone you claim has jewelry in it and find another intricate brain, you say. But that, I say, would underscore my thesis: since that person's skull would have been opened, of course chances are you would find a brain in it. That does not dispute my assertion that finding a brain is mere coincidence. Ditto with CAT-scan. The next person whose head you crack might have a skull filled with snowberries and zinnias. With miniature dogs, pugs and poodles. Pewits, terns, finches.

17. LOVE STORY

Julius Marx, great curmudgeon, stogie and a bushy mustache with some small black eyes stuck on it, ebony glasses, Groucho by trade, hunched by nature, lived in California. Tom Eliot, Missourian, English accent transplanted onto his own, lived in London. After years of witty, shining correspondence, they finally met for dinner and discovered they had nothing to say to one another. They even failed at small talk. Julius made polite excuses and left early.

18. A SHORT STORY

He ravaged her.

19. WHY IS THIS HOW I ACT?

Last night I was dreaming I was dreaming. I was flying at terrific velocity among red brick tenements, arms extended, naked. Hundreds of clotheslines were strung between the buildings. On these clotheslines hung thousands of sheets, towels, socks, underwear, stockings, blouses, jeans, sneakers. Somehow I couldn't pull up. I kept jetting into the clothes, getting all tangled up. Bras caught in my mouth. Cutoffs blinded me. Pillow cases wrapped around my head. I couldn't scream, of course.

20. WHAT DO YOU WANT US TO DO?

We understand you're a very private person, Gilby. We understand you probably wait by your answering machine and listen to our messages as we speak them. We believe you're listening right now. We have discussed this and agree we're okay with it. We respect your choices. But, um, did we miss something? Overlook some detail? Were we unconsciously cruel? Unconsciously kind? If so, we apologize straight from the heart. We never meant to hurt you, Gilby. We never meant to help you, either. Just tell us what you want us to do. Tell us to jump. Sit. Tell us to love each other harder.

21. LOVE STORY

Hi Gilby. I'm pregnant. You're the father.

22. MOTORCARS

It is quite sure that motorcars don't grow out of the earth, Wittgenstein reminded himself on paper. The man who followed films starring Carmen Miranda with a gentle yet inexorable passion, the man who died of cancer while reading *Black Beauty* at his doctor's house, smiled. Here was something he could be sure of. In celebration he walked outside into a blue Sunday afternoon, calculated the height of the maple in front of his house by pacing off from the trunk the base of a right triangle, wheeling around and sighting along his walking stick.

Tell them I've had a wonderful life, were his last words.

23. BUMHOLE

You're a bumhole, Gilby. A ninnyhammer. A cluck, a gowk, a gaby, a fud. You're a looby, a bufflehead, a dunderpate, a clot. A swag and a bindlestiff. A bindlestiff, Gilby. A goddamn bindlestiff.

24. WHAT'S MY LINE?

Okay okay okay: I just don't know what to say anymore. I can change, by the way. I don't have any big theory about the stability of selfhood over time or anything. I can add several inches to my height. Losing weight has never been a problem for me. Or putting it on. I can put it on, too. Dye my hair. Un–dye it. Sometimes I stand there looking at myself in the mirror and I say: How does Gilby see me? How would Gilby like to see me? I stick a pillow under my shirt. I use that styling mousse that turns my hair orange and makes me look startled. It goes without saying I can brush my teeth more often. I can be much less successful in my life. Or much more successful. Your choice. But you already know that. I can aspire to greater things, needless to say, watch more TV or less, criticize *Elle,* use the word *postmodern* with greater frequency in my discourse to refer to objects such as ski jackets, staplers, coffee mugs, cuisine that employs a purplish element, novels that employ shopping lists and recipes, music that makes it easy for you to fall asleep, hats no one would wear, the general sense I have lately that

25. ON CERTAINTY
This isn't working so well, is it.

26. TWO FEET
True story. Cemetery. Blanching grass. Faceless crowd. Funeral for Charles Olson, the man who stuffed food in his pockets at dinner parties and once ate an oil rag. Allen Ginsberg chanting Kaddish even though he isn't one-hundred-percent sure of the pronunciation. Not paying attention to what he's doing, Ginsberg accidentally trips on the pedal that lowers the alcoholic bear's coffin into the grave. An unstoppable mechanical hum follows. Ginsberg stops chanting and looks down at what his feet have done. The coffin has not been aligned before its descent and so jams cockeyed, half in, half out. The funeral stops. Henceforth Ginsberg vehemently denies such an event ever actually took place. In what sense is he right?

27. TEN QUESTION MARKS
What is your favorite color? Who do you like to read these days? What's your new girlfriend like? Your old one? What is the relationship between space and time when considered in terms of a Hegelian dialectic? Do you still like pistachio ice cream? What did Bataille mean when he said the sexual act is in time what the tiger is in space? Seen any good films lately? Catch the latest Academy Awards? What do you think about the latest incident in the Middle East? Did you want Cher to win?

28. FEELING REDUNDANT FEELING REDUNDANT

I'm going to leave you alone now, Gilby. I'm beginning to feel like a human tautology. I hate that.

29. THE ONE YOU WERE WAITING FOR

Okay, so. I'm not going to leave you alone. But almost. A little more every morning. Until one day you'll rewind your answering machine and hit play and listen to a string of disembodied voices, and the one you won't hear will be mine.

30. SUNDAY AFTERNOON

We must remember certain things. I just called to tell you. We have to preserve the fragrance of those apples, for instance. Licorice. Nightmares. They way that evening beneath the maple you reached out and touched me with your fingers just below my left eye. The precise second the red-gold sunlight flashed in your hair and my heart went stupid and a robin darted into my consciousness and I thought if there is a perfect moment, if there is a breath-catching instant, this is it. How wrong could I have been?

Small but Significant Invasions

MOUCHE AND I INVITE THEM OVER for cocktails early one July evening. We only glance at each other when they show up lugging suitcases. Perhaps Mouche grins at me over her shoulder as we lead them through the hot gray corridors of our house and out onto the back porch into the scream of cicadas. They are laughing, making jokes about the season. Mouche goes for the gin-and-tonics while we three sit down in wicker chairs and watch dry blue lightning silently split the sky. We talk about the lingering humidity. About the scholarly book on which he is working: a project to establish the provenance of four 16th-century paintings that no longer exist except as references in various historical texts. The whole time I sit with my knees pressed together, moist palms flat on my kneecaps. A clatter comes down a hallway and Mouche appears balancing four cloudy glasses on a silver tray. She wears a t-shirt with a picture of Monet stamped across the front and a pair of faded jean shorts. Her shoulders are a smooth brown. I wear a pair of white jogging shorts and an undershirt, no shoes. The couple is wearing suits. He wears a khaki sports coat and khaki pants and Birkenstocks and a green knit shirt with a tiny white polo player whacking a ball over the pocket. She wears a red sports coat of some thin summer material and a matching dress and red high heels. I glance at Mouche as if to say: So what can you do? She glances back at me as if to say: Not a whole bunch. Neither of us enjoys having guests over because something like this invariably happens. We are either overdressed or underdressed, too tight-laced or not tight-laced enough. So I sit with my knees together and my moist palms flat on my kneecaps, trying to remember if on the phone I indicated to them this was in some way supposed to be a special event.

We chat for a while and then he suggests we play a game. No one makes mention of supper and yet it is past eight and my stomach has begun to hiss and gurgle. For the better part of the next hour we recite punch lines, trying to find our way back to the original joke.

No soap radio.

We may now perhaps to begin, yes?

Around nine Mouche perks up.

Say, she says, feigning casualness, could we interest you in a bite to eat? We have the makings for some sandwiches. Bologna…

That would be lovely, if it's not too much trouble, the woman says.

Mouche disappears. The woman smiles. I smile. The man leans over, picks up my copy of *The Courtier* from the bookshelf forming a wall beside him and begins thumbing through it.

A stranger looking in on this scene would be led to believe nothing were out of the ordinary.

After dinner the woman excuses herself and heads upstairs. The man and I stroll leisurely into the living room. He takes a seat in the leather chair beneath our unicorn tapestry poster, flicks on a nearby light, returns to *The Courtier* in a hot yellow circle. I sit on the piano stool, pick through some music. Outside the cicadas are furious. A stagnant wet heat has settled over everything. Blue lightning flickers and frogs croak frantically down by the swamp. A damp scent, hint of mildew in it, pushes through the hot gray corridors; the dining room with its French doors open wide to the night; the library with its heavy smell of dank pages and musk; the three large bedrooms upstairs with their massive oak furniture carrying the fragrance of saturated wood and the moist bedspreads and unclean sheets; the bathroom with the sniff of rust and old water in the air.

A while and I get up and wander through the dark house, thinking, discovering myself in a long passageway and then in the incredibly brilliant light of the kitchen, watching Mouche wash the dishes. Her bottom is firm and wonderful. Several pubic hairs curl out the left leg of her shorts; she has forgotten to shave. She turns around and I see a dew of perspiration on her forehead, in the fine fuzz above her upper lip. A strand of hair clings to her right temple. I brush it back. There is a quietness pressing in that it seems criminal to fracture, so we speak in low voices.

What time is it? I ask.

Almost eleven.

We should do something, watch television or something. I think they're getting bored.

I'm really tired, Mouche says.

She rests her head against my chest, fresh scent of her hair rising around me. I hug her and look up at the bright light.

Just a little longer, okay?

I am so proud of her it is nearly impossible to express. When I return to the living room I notice he's still alone. I ask where she's gone.

Bed, he says, adds: She's getting tired easier in her old age.

He laughs.

I laugh too.

Sure enough she is draped across our bed, still dressed, her suit hiked up over her waist. Her suitcase is open on our oak armoire. Black lace underwear. Black lace bra. Deodorant can. Makeup kit smudged with pinks and greens and blues. A thick-toothed comb. Brush. A tube of toothpaste, clear green fluid dripping out. I go down to the kitchen to tell Mouche, but can't find her there. I check the porch, wander through the garden out back, poke my head into the living room (he is still reading), walk the corridors searching. *Mouche?* I whisper. *Mouche? Mouche?* There's no light whatsoever in the interior now. I bump into things. A plant falls and smashes. I pause and listen. In the distance a rumble. Thunder perhaps. *Mouche? Mouche?* I push open an oak door, climb a flight of stairs, walk down the long stifling hall that leads to the back. In one passageway I think I hear something; stop; wait; call out. But it's nothing, the grumble of a pipe maybe. I stand wiping my nose. I can't find light switches to orient myself. It could be eleven-thirty or four in the morning. I give up my search, lie down on the thick carpeting, rest my head on my arms.

We live with them through the summer, more than once having to confess to ourselves they are pleasant housemates. She is remarkably clean, helps us tidy every room (except our bedroom, in which she sleeps) and he is no trouble at all. He spends much of his time composing his monograph in the living room or thumbing through books in the library.

Although Mouche and I seldom speak with them, they with us, there is something cordial in the atmosphere. We celebrate Labor Day together, Mouche cooking up a pot roast, smooth mashed potatoes, green peas, steamed carrots. All the vegetables are from our garden out back. We watch the football game together on Thanksgiving, drive out into the forest to locate a small pine tree for Christmas. Early in December the winter rains come, bringing with them a wet coolness and thousands of glistening black frogs. We start up the fireplaces and sit around, Mouche's head on my lap, watching the flames eat the wood, sip creme de cacao in warm milk. Mouche and I sleep in the living room on the carpet so we can tend the fire at night. In the spring we climb into the flowing mud, fast streams sweeping through our yard, and commence the long slow process of shoveling away frog corpses, re-digging ditches in order to channel off the water. We plant again, prune the banana, orange, lemon, lime trees. For Easter Mouche bakes an angel cake. We sit at the dining room table, a cool breeze coming through the French doors and laugh and drink gin-and-tonics and tell stories until our heads spin. Mouche grins over the brim of her glass at me. I sit at the table with my knees together and poke the bobbing ice cubes in my glass, playing with the sparkles, listening to the tinkles as delicate as Chinese chimes.

One day in June Mouche catches cold and remains inside, in the living room, wrapped to the chin in an Indian blanket, while I work in the garden. I kneel and chop, knead and dig, thoughtless. Hours waft up and away like balloons. The sun turns the sky a mad blue. Birds, dull gray and brown, noise the branches. A healthy perspiration trickles down my face, neck, spine. I collect pile after pile of weeds with incredibly long and slender white roots, concentrating on the movement of my hands—my knuckles grimy with soil, my fingernails black crescents of humus.

When the sun disappears behind the house I stand and return the shovel, trowel and aluminum bucket to the shed. I try the back door and realize it's locked. I jimmy the doorknob. Nothing happens. Knock at the porch door. No one answers. I walk around front and ring the bell, wait several seconds, ring again. I try the porch door again.

Mouche! I shout. Mouche!

I trot around to the French doors and find them locked, too. I try the windows. I rap against the glass panes, kick against the base of the house, jog around back.

Mouche! I shout. *Open the door! Open the door!*

I lean against the window, cupping my hands and peering in. The house is dark. I can't make out anything as colors fade around me. I remain there, looking in from time to time, for much of the night.

Next morning a hot white haze hangs over the garden. The thick air smells of roses. I lie on my side drifting in and out of sleep beneath a back window. My ribs are throbbing and then the porch door is clapping shut and there is the clump-clump-clump of footsteps.

Mouche's eyes are puffy with sleep. She walks right by me, saying over her shoulder: Come on, let's get going.

Going?

I look over at the porch door.

They locked it behind me. Windows too. I'm hungry. Let's eat and get going.

Which is what we do—sit in the garden amidst mimosa and hyacinth and make a small feast of bananas. After a while we exchange looks and stand and head out. We cut through the yard and onto the street. Hand in hand, we stroll past many houses that have been taken over and some that have not.

FROM

Sewing Shut My Eyes

(2000)

Cybermorphic Beat-Up Get-Down
Subterranean Homesick Reality-Sandwich Blues

I'M A, LIKE, POET. MONA. MONA SAUSALITO. I write lyrics for my boyfriend's band, Plato's Deathmetal Tumors. Plato's Deathmetal Tumors kicks butt. It's one of the best Neogoth bands in Seattle. My boyfriend's name is Mosh. Mosh shaved his head and tattooed it with rad circuitry patterns. He plays wicked cool lead and sings like Steve Tyler on amphetamines. Only that's not his real name. His real name is Marvin Goldstein. Anyway. Like I say, I'm a poet. I write about human sacrifices, cannibalism, vampires, and stuff. Mosh loves my work. He says we're all going to be famous some day. Only right now we're not, which bites, cuz I've been writing for almost like ten months. These things take time, I guess. Except we need some, like, cash to get by from week to week? Which is why Mosh one day says take the job at Escort à la Mode. Why not? I say. Which I guess kind of brings me to my story.

See, I'm cruising Capitol Hill in one of the company's black BMWs when my phone rings. Escort à la Mode's a real high-class operation. Escortette's services go for $750 an hour. We usually work with foreign business types. Japs and ragheads mostly. Politicians, too. With 24 hours' notice we can also supply bogus daughters, brothers, and sons. Except there's absolutely nothing kinky here. We don't even kiss the clients. Handshakes max. Take them out, show them the town, eat at a nice restaurant, listen to them yak, take them to a club, watch them try to dance, take them home. Period. We're tour guides, like. Our goal is to make people feel interesting. Therma Payne—she's my boss—Therma says our job is to *give good consort*. Therma's a scream.

But so. Like I say, my phone rings. Dispatcher gives me an address, real rank bookstore called Hard Covers down by the fish market. My client's supposed to be this hot-shit writer guy who's reading there. Poet. Famous back in like the Pleistocene Error or something. So important I never heard of him. But, hey. It's a job.

Now I'm not being like unmodest or anything, okay? But I happen to be fucking gorgeous. My skin's überwhite. I dye my hair, which is short and spiked, shoe-polish black, then streak it with these little pink wisps. Which picks up my Lancôme Corvette-red lipstick and long Estée Lauder Too-Good-To-Be-Natural black lashes. When I talk with a client, I'll keep my eyes open real wide so I always look Winona-Ryder-surprised by what he's saying. I'm 5'2", and when I wear my Number Four black-knit body-dress and glossy black Mouche army boots I become every middle-aged man's bad-little-girl wet dream. So I don't just *walk* in to Hard Covers, okay? I kind of, what, *sashay*. Yeah. That's it. *Sashay*. I've never been there before, and I'm frankly pretty fucking impressed. Place is just *humongous*. More a warehouse than bookstore. Except that it's all mahogany and bronze and carpeting. Health-food bar. Espresso counter. Dweeb with bat-wing ears playing muzak at the baby grand. Area off on the side with a podium and loads of chairs for the reading. Which is already filling. Standing room only. People all excited and shit. And books. Jesus Hitler Christ. Books. Enough books to make you instantly anxious you'll never read them all, no way, no matter how hard you try, so you mind as well not.

I'm right on time. So I ask the guy at the register for the famous rich poet. He points to the storeroom. Warming up, he says. So I go on back and knock, only no one answers. I knock again. Nada. My meter's running, and I figure I mind as well earn my paycheck, so I try the knob. Door's unlocked. I open it, stick my head in, say hi. It's pretty dark, all shadows and book cartons, and the room stretches on for like forever, and I'm already getting bored, so I go on in. When my eyes adjust a little I make out a dim light way off in this distant corner. I start weaving toward it through the rows of cartons. As I get closer I can hear these voices. They sound kind of funny. Worried, like. Real fast and low. And then I see them. I see the whole thing.

Maybe five or six guys in gray business suits and ties, real FBI or whatever, huddling over this jumble on the floor. At first I don't understand what I'm looking at. Then I make out the portable gurney. And this torso on it, just this *torso*, naked and fleshy pink in a doll sort of way, rib cage big as a cow's, biggest fucking belly you ever saw. Out of it are sticking these skinny white flabby legs, between them this amazingly small little purple dick and two hairy marbles. Only, thing is, the chest isn't a real chest? There's a panel in it. And the panel's open. And one of the guys is tinkering with some wiring in there. And another is rummaging through a wooden crate, coming up with an arm, plugging it into the torso, while a third guy, who's been balancing a second arm over his shoulder like a rifle or something, swings it down and locks it into place.

Okay. Look. I may be a poet and all, but I'm not a fucking liar or anything. I'm telling you what I saw. Believe it or not. Frankly I don't give a shit. I'm standing there, hypnotized like, not sure whether to run or wet myself, when this fourth guy reaches into the crate and comes up with, I kid you not, the *head*. I swear. I fucking swear. A *head*. The thing is so gnarly. Pudgy. Bushy. Gray-haired. And with these *eyes*. With these sort of glazed *eyes* that're looking up into the darkness where the ceiling should've been.

Anyway, after a pretty long time fidgeting with the stuff in the chest, they prop the torso into a sitting position and start attaching the head. It's not an easy job. They fiddle and curse, and once one of them slips with a screwdriver and punctures the thing's left cheek. Only they take some flesh-toned putty or whatever and fill up the hole. And the third guy reaches into his breast pocket and produces these wire-rimmed glasses, which he slips into place on the thing's face, and then they stand back, arms folded, admiring their work and all, and then the first guy reaches behind the thing's neck and pushes what must've been the ON/OFF button.

Those eyes roll down and snap into focus. Head swivels side to side. Mouth opens and closes its fatty lips, testing. And then, shit, man, it begins *talking*. It begins fucking *talking*.

I'm with you in Rockland. I'm wuh-wuh-wuh-with you … But my agent. What sort of agent is that? What could she have been thinking? Have you seen those sales figures? A stone should have better than that! I'm wuh-with you in the nightmare of trade paperbacks, sudden flash of bad PR, suffering the outrageousness of weak blurbs and failing shares. Where is the breakthrough book? The advance? Share with me the vanity of the unsolicited manuscript! Show me the madman bum of a publicist! Movie rights! Warranties! Indemnities! I am the twelve percent royalty! I am the first five-thousand copies! I am the retail and the wholesale, the overhead and the option clause! Give me the bottom line! Give me the tax break! Give me a reason to collect my rough drafts in the antennae crown of commerce! Oh, mental, mental, mental hardcover! Oh, incomplete clause! Oh, hopeless abandon of the unfulfilled contract! I'm wuh-wuh-wuh-with you ... I'm wuh-wuh-wuh-with you in Rockland ... I'm ...

Oh, shit, says the first guy.

Balls, says the second.

We should've let him go, says the third.

When his ticker stopped, says the first.

When his liver quit, says the second.

One thing, says the fourth. Nanotech sure the fuck ain't what it's cracked up to be.

Got that right, says the third.

Thirty thousand books in 1998 alone, the famous rich poet says, *but they couldn't afford it. Tangier, Venice, Amsterdam. What were they thinking? Wall Street is holy! The New York Stock Exchange is holy! The cosmic clause is holy! I'm wuh-wuh-wuh ... I'm wuh-wuh-wuh ... wuh-wuh-wuh ...*

Turn him off, says the fourth one.

Pale greenish foam begins forming on the famous rich poet's lips, dribbling down his chin, spattering his hairless chest.

Yeah, well, says the second.

Guess we got some tightening to do, says the third, reaching behind the thing's neck.

But just as he pressed that button, just for a fraction of an instant, the stare of the famous rich poet fell on me as I tried scrunching out of sight behind this wall of boxes. Our eyes met. His looked like those of a wrongly convicted murderer maybe one second before the executioner throws the switch that'll send a quadrillion volts sizzling through his system. In them was this mixture of disillusionment, dismay, deeply fucked-up fear, and uninterrupted sorrow. I froze. He stretched his foam-filled mouth as wide as it would go, ready to bellow, ready to howl. Except the juice failed. His mouth slowly closed again. His eyes rolled back up inside his head.

And me?

I said *fuck this*. Fuck the books, fuck the suits, fuck Escort à la Mode, fuck the withered old pathetic shit. This whole thing's *way* too fucking rich for *my* blood.

And so I turned and walked.

Strategies in the Overexposure
of Well-Lit Space

237. THE DISCOVERY: CHANNEL

Kerwin Penumbro, who's taking off his birthday from his job designing and manufacturing certain popular body organs (greasy heart still breathing in a madman's fist is it almost goes without saying a perennial favorite, though you should never underestimate the power of a bluish-white intestines wrapped around a startled housewife's fire poker) at the small special effects house just off Pioneer Square in Seattle, is expecting maybe a beige sweater with maroon stripes, or one of those Timex watches that lets you know the hour in Australia and Greenland simultaneously and is water-resistant down to like a hundred meters, from his girlfriend, Syndi Shogunn, who Ker met four years ago in front of the remainders bin at that just-slightly-kinked record store a block over, The Vinyl Fetish (Ker looking for the esoteric compilation on Air Pyrate Muzzik containing every pertinent Beatles song played backwards, *Re-Volver*, while Syndi, a secretary over at the local police station, ferreted for a disc housing themes to all those really great action-adventures-with-even-a-vague-connection-to-law-enforcement on the tube from the late sixties and early seventies to enhance her workplace ambiance ... those golden years that brought you *I Spy, Mannix, Mission Impossible, The Man From U.N.C.L.E., Batman, The Fugitive* ... a-and even those truly warped masterpieces like *The Prisoner*, if you stretched your operational definitions a little ... Syndi able to just go on and on about such things), but no way the knock on their apartment door this Thursday morning, Syndi away at the office for the day, coffee prickling the air ... not the May sun in Ker's rattled eyes ... and certainly not the two men in khaki shirts, khaki pants, and five-o'clock stubble at maybe nine o'clock in the a.m. standing next to the slim cardboard box nearly six feet tall and four wide, saying: Mr. Penumbro? We got your TV here . . .

212. IMMORTALITY: STEALTH

A–and not your standard TV, either. This baby is gargantuan and looks like it's been designed in a wind tunnel. It's made out of smooth black plastic and has lots of curves everywhere and Kerwin could under the right circumstances imagine it flying.

Plus it's the best of best models: the renowned Mitsubishi Stealth.

Plus it comes with one of those incredible mini-satellite deals you hook up outside your window and get like a bazillion channels on.

Kerwin Penumbro, TV-less for the better part of a decade, falls in love with Syndi Shogunn all over again.

While he's doing so the delivery people search for the optimum viewing area, 7.4 feet to 13.6 feet from the screen, hook up the cable, set the tuning mode to AUTO position, flick the STEREO/MONO switch to STEREO, toy with the convergence panel, the quick-view, the remote.

Instead of breakfast, Ker sits in his beanbag chair in the middle of the living room like a king in his bamboo throne on a South Pacific island (he's wearing only his grayish jockey shorts, which he knows as well as anyone should really undergo a good washing about now) and studies his owner's manual.

In place of the nap he planned to take sometime before noon, he makes himself a monstrous bologna birthday sandwich with lettuce, tomatoes, pickles, a wedge of onion, mustard, and even this serious dollop of mayo (the expiration date on the jar barely noticeably out of fashion) on top of which he sprinkles cashews and what's left of his jelly-bean stash, tears open a bag of O'Boise potato chips, and flips the top of a Bud, collapses in his threadbare beanbag chair 8.3 feet from the black monolith, squirms toward comfort, and clicks the ON button the femtosecond the delivery people close the door behind them.

Clicks the OFF button.

Stands, trots into the bedroom, rifles through his sock drawer, finds his last Baby Ruth, shnorks it for an improved disposition on the way back to the living room, fidgets into his beanbag chair like John Glenn into Friend-ship 7, clicks the ON button.

Clicks the OFF button.

Stands, trots into the bathroom, thumbs down the front of his Fruit of the Looms, relaxes his urethra, stares at the high-gloss ceiling (across which scrolls a single robotic ant) while listening with pride to the vigorous plash-ing below, wriggles himself dry, pops the front of his Fruit of the Looms into place, whistling without really realizing he's whistling (the reverse ver-sion of *Strawberry Fields*), feels the sugar from the Baby Ruth beginning to itch the glassy horizon of his brain, trots back to the living room, fidgets into this beanbag chair, chomps into his sandwich, clicks the ON button.

Clicks the OFF button.

Stands, trots into the bedroom, throws on a pair of jeans and sneakers and a Sick Poppies t-shirt (black woodcut of a sleeping head, python-long tongue lolling out and curling below like a garden hose, on a white back-ground), trots into the kitchen, searches the top drawer beside the stove for his keys, grabs his black denim jacket in whose pocket he knows resides every penny he possesses for the remainder of the month (more than two weeks to go . . . a-and how did *that* happen?), jogs onto the porch, down the external wooden staircase, down the block to the 7-Eleven where he purchases a pint of Cherry Garcia from an underfed guy with a lightning-bolt scar zagged across his forehead.

Jogs up the block, up the external wooden staircase, onto the porch, into the kitchen, down the hall, back to the kitchen where he picks up a spoon and deposits said keys and jacket, down the hall again, into the living room, into the beanbag chair, and, panting, clicks the ON button once more.

350. PRIME: TIME: LIVE
Kerwin Penumbro experiences his consciousness expand in a flood of su-crose-enhanced light.

141. DUCK & COVER
Nona Nova, hospital nurse, has battled illness on the eleven-to-seven shift. She has shocked a cardiac victim back from the brink of death; uncovered a plot by fiendish candy-striper Stephanie Stix to kill elderly patients; eased

Dale Devin, young doctor, from his depression brought on by his wife Dolly's abscondence, a pending malpractice suit, and by his youngest son, little Donny Devin, dying in a freak fiery plane crash in the Andes (fog, tribal blow-gun competition); cheered up a child laced with tumors; unraveled the labyrinthine financial problems gnawing at Dustin Elwood, hospital head. Nona is thus understandably tired. Her legs feel like hardening cement. Her head feels like twelve feet under a swimming pool. Her body feels old at twenty-seven. She stands in the restroom, staring forlornly in the mirror at the mulberry sleep-bruises gathered below her methylene-blue eyes, unzips her uniform, reveals her tight belly, almond-brown skin, pert breasts barely hidden under bra. She runs warm water in the sink. Splashes her face. Reaches for a handful of paper towels. Only when she looks in the mirror again another head floats behind hers: Rex Rory, flamboyant resident. Nona Nova ducks and covers.

246. CARTOON GEL: HOMELESSNESS: LIGHT

Kerwin Penumbro claps in unabashed delight, forgetting he's holding the bologna sandwich, which pretty much negates itself across his lap. Unfazed, he reconstructs it best he can and takes another bite.

Because it's like living in a cartoon gel, the colors are so bright, the outlines so crisp. Everything is animation rich.

A-and the sound . . . the sound is . . . Ker believes he feels spittle collecting along his lower lip.

Which totally undercuts the theory he developed as a philosophy major for his undergraduate honors thesis, which states that imagination and desire continually outstrip technology . . . as in we're always waiting for the transistors to catch up with our synapses, always able to out-think the next mechanical or digital advance.

Nope.

He was wrong.

This just about does it.

Though, true, nonetheless, that, well . . . look at computers. If your basic car advanced at the same rate your basic computer did over the past two decades, you'd be looking at a vehicle that travels at five-hundred-thousand miles an hour, gets a million miles to the gallon, and costs less than a down payment on a Stealth like this. Which is simply to say things have gotten pretty . . . what. Fun. Weird. Fun. For instance, look at Ker looking at himself looking at the box, Ker thinks, looking. You'd imagine he was watching a really interesting sex arrangement through a one-way mirror when in fact he is watching this maybe awful soap opera that he simply can't turn away from.

Culture's first perceptual orifice, his theory goes, which is in fact some-one else's theory, he's pretty sure, was your no-frills cave door: primary purpose of allowing hominidal passage.

Culture's second, once we'd gotten beyond those load-bearing external walls, was, natch, the window: primary purpose of facilitating movement of light and air.

And but culture's third window?

Well, you're looking at it.

Or looking at Ker looking at himself look at it, except you don't look *out* through the third window. You look *in*. But the *in* you're looking at pretends it's an *out*, which it sometimes is, sort of, if you think about it. Plus it's not so much that *you* look in or out as *it* looks in or out, kind of borrowing your eyes from you and every now and then forgetting to give them back. Plus what it does, honestly, is to bring stuff outside inside, such as it is, though the outside stuff pretends to be outside stuff when it's actually inside stuff, as in produced and edited and so forth, and though it makes you feel you're always somewhere else when you're in truth always doing nothing much more than, like Ker here, feeling the spittle form on your lower lip while participating in the rampant over-exposure of well-lit space, taking another bite of your sandwich in a world without borders, because your home becomes someone else's home, your digital front door always being open, and not exactly yours, even while it *is* yours . . .

Which is to say nothing of stuff like email a-and smart phones a-and iPads a-and . . .

Ker interrupts himself to wonder if he's really heard, or only imagined he's heard, that there exists a model of the Mitsubishi Stealth that comes with a catheter for a prolonged viewing experience.

118. ROSES: TEACUP: REVOLVER

You no good varmint! the barrel-chested man in the white cowboy hat at the breakfast table proclaims. Three roses in a crystal vase. White tablecloth. Beflowered china. Tinkle of teacups. *You polecat! You think you can plan my daddy's downfall and get away with it? You think you can sabotage his oil wells and mama and me'd sit still for it? Lickin' my boots is too good for you.*

The barrel-chested man in the black cowboy hat smirks.

An what you gonna do about it? he asks.

This! the barrel-chested man in the white cowboy hat shouts, flipping an oily blue revolver into view.

498. HE LEARNS HOW TO LOSE GRACEFULLY

Rope-and-log bridge wobbling over ravine.

Skydiver in red, white, and blue jumpsuit. Lightning bolts on his helmet. Parachute on his back. Flawless teeth in his grin. He raises two fingers to his forehead in a flip salute to posterity, gingerly climbs over the cable, poises, arches his back, leaps toward the river threading below.

He plummets like a starfish.

You wait one one-thousand, two one-thousand, three.

He plummets like a car heading through the railing in a thriller.

Except there is no white bouquet of chute, no slowing of momentum, no noise save the whipping of wind far above the tiny red, white, and blue dot.

You watch him begin to flap his arms, a little at first, then harder and harder.

177. UNCLE BUDDY'S PHANTOM FUNHOUSE

Teenagers believe they are immortal, says this Rod-Serlingesque voice as the camera pans through the wooded night, which is clearly a Hollywood day seen through a special filter, fake car lights wobbling through fake pines on a lonely fake gravel road. *They believe nothing will ever happen to them as they live on their own psychic planet in a world where deodorant, hair style, jeans length, acoustic preference, and mouthwash products matter deeply. They sleep profoundly, having all the dreams they should have. But these five teenagers on their way to a desolate farmhouse somewhere in upstate New York, who are under the false impression they are moving through a sexual and psychic rite of passage called A Weekend at Uncle Buddy's Hunting Cabin involving alcohol, tobacco, and fire arms, will die before dawn, and horribly, one by one, mostly in nothing save their underwear, their breaths a hive of plaque and pre-gingivital fear at the hands of*

283. RUBBER WIG: CHILDBIRTH: HOMICIDE

I's a killer, announces weeping Bobbie Joe Sue Alice Mary Bobson, who according to the ID at the bottom of the screen is a seamstress living in a trailer park in northwestern Florida.

Her hair reminds Kerwin of whipped cream in its hue and shape.

She will be buried in a piano case, it occurs to him, she's so fat.

Share your pain with us, urges psychic healer Abbey Rode, whose hair reminds Kerwin of a red rubber wig. Abbey has that slack-muscled serious-yet-utterly-accepting face that only drugged children, Southern preachers, morticians, and talk-show psychic healers have.

We're here for you, she says, reaching out and patting Bobbie Joe Sue Alice Mary on the wrist.

Bobbie Joe Sue Alice Mary snorfles.

My stepfather and his minister done abused my second cousin Pattie Bob Anne Frankie Patson when she was eleven and done got her with child.

Pan to empathetic audience faces riveted by the drama unfolding before them.

What happened next?

I didn't find none of this out till last year. Only one night I's sittin' in my hot tub out back with my boyfriend Billy Ray Tom John, and Billy Ray Tom John? He turns to me and says somethin' real rude about my weight displacing all the water and pretty much emptyin' the tub out, so I's feel liken to kill him. And then it all comes afloodin' back, so I's calls the Psychic Healer Hotline.

Dhambala be thanked.

Snorfle snorfle snorfle.

… ?

And then you and me, we come to meet and all and you undresses me to my former life, only afore we get there I take this what you call it detour and sees me afloatin' in my momma's womb … only I's not alone.

… ?

I's got me a twin brother I ain't never knowed about. And then I start rememberin' how he done raped me inside there, how I become my twin-brother fetus's sex slave. Only I starts aplannin'. Float and watch. Float and watch. And I's wait till he's asleepin, and I real careful like just reach over and slip his umbilical cord round his neck. Never forgets the way his eyes sorta popped open.

222. PLAY: SIN

Not long ago our culture believed play was tantamount to wasting time, this avuncular voice narrates, *a distraction from the important matters that kept a society whole and functioning. Some regarded it as a punishable sin, the devil's work that chipped away at serious moral pursuits. But now most psychologists believe play is a necessary part of growing up. It helps children develop healthy attitudes and bodies. It paradoxically instills a sense of rule following and allows children a chance to vent excess energy. Recreational activities teach children to get along with others. The personality of a child grows as he or she learns new skills and develops confidence in sports—motor, sensory, or intellectual. In competitive games, he or she learns how to lose gracefully.*

259. THE GREAT WHEEL SPINS

The great wheel spins. The audience shouts. The game show host becomes his mouth full of teeth. Mabel Utta, sixty-two, from Dayton, Ohio, with a son in the Navy, jumps up and down, fat chugging, and claps her tiny hands in glee.

203. ART: CRIMES

Yeah, well, um … this is? We startin.? … What? Oh. My name is … my working name is Zondi. No. Just Zondi. Fuck the parental-naming thing. That's all about social control and shit. I was raised in Hackensack, New Jersey. I live in the East Village. Yeah. I'm a performance artist … what? Yeah. I knew it was my calling for like fuckingever. When I was thirteen or something? I saw this thing in this underground zine about this woman who performed surgery on herself and televised the operations around the world. I forget her name. She's dead. Liver transplant. Anyway, so I knew then I had what it took to be a cultural practitioner. ... What? Oh, so no, the fucking capitalist art establishment wouldn't accept me. Fucking tight-assed fuckheads. I couldn't get in to even like art school. They said I didn't have no talent cuz I couldn't draw or paint or nothing. I'm a fucking cultural practitioner. I've had to pay all my life. So I majored in communications. They flunked me in math and social sciences and composition and a couple of other things I forget. Which is what took me to the city, where I met Mongo. ... What? Right. Just Mongo. He thinks and everything. He once studied with that guy. And so he introduced me to the idea of AIDS ... Arts In Denial & Shit ... which it deals with art that denies it's art, only that gave me the idea for my magum okus. ... What? Nineteen. ... What? One-point-two million. Yeah. So anyways, I go to myself: fuck the commodrification of the arts and the fascist market. Fuck art dealers who wipe their asses with the masters like, you know, everybody. And so right there in this nice café in the East Village this cool post-strucuralistic concept of my magum okus hits me: NOT. Get it? ... What? So I decide I won't create a fucking thing for the rest of my life. *That's* my project. It's an act of negation deal, like. Defiance. No paintings, no sculptures, no lithographs, no videos, no mobiles, no prints, no assemblages, no collages, no sketches, no nothing. ... What? What you *think* it means? ... What? Sleep late. Listen to tunes. Last year I took up sailing ... right after I joined that yacht club thing over on Long Island, which is pretty cool. I really like TV. Cartoons, mostly. ... What? No, I don't miss it. Lately I've been thinking about taking up teaching. I figure maybe it's time to start giving something back.

249. SHE LEARNS HOW TO LOSE GRACEFULLY

She's already tired. Her body feels old at nineteen. She stands in the back bedroom on the first floor of Uncle Buddy's Hunting Cabin and stares forlornly at herself in the mirror. Tom isn't the gentleman she'd imagined. Or maybe Tim is the gentleman she *had* imagined. Sometimes it's hard to tell. She unzips her jeans, skins them off, shrugs her Sick Poppies t-shirt over her head. Runs warm water in the shower. Her breasts beneath her lace bra. Reaches for the Ivory soap on the sink ledge. Her breasts beneath her lace brace. Her name is Melinda. Or maybe it's Belinda or Brenda. Ker either wasn't paying attention when it was mentioned or it wasn't mentioned while he was paying attention. When Melinda or Belinda or Brenda looks in the steamy mirror again another head floats behind hers.

Zodiac Killer, homicidal maniac. Bright brown eyes. Flawless teeth in the mouth hole of his ski mask. He raises two fingers to his forehead in a flip salute to posterity. The first teenager, wearing lace panties and bra, ducks and covers. An ice pick glints in the shadows above her fourteen gallons of bleached-blond hair. She opens her mouth to scream. The ice pick descends.

The first teenager senses mortality.

201. THE DISCOVERY: CHANNEL

Uh, hey … Ker says, beer can pausing maybe two centimeters from his lips.

He leans forward.

Wasn't that … yeah … wasn't that *Syndi's* face in the audience-reaction shot back there? Okay, so maybe it took a couple of minutes to register, but there it was, wasn't it, just after that what's-her-name, that lady with the whipped-cream hair, admitted she whacked her own fraternal twin in utero.

He leans back.

Okay, Take Two: there was this anorexic mom-type with green turtle-shell glasses next to a black rodential woman with simpatico tears in her eyes … a-and right behind them, bobbing just out of focus, was … Ker'd of course recognize her anywhere … long honey hair in a ponytail … wire-rimmed glasses … slightly puzzled eyes … almost like Ker wasn't the only one wondering why she was where she was …

Only … why *was* she there? Supposed to be at work today. Plus that show was shot … where? New York, probably. Maybe Chicago or L.A.

Ker shudders.

Well, these things were always prerecorded, weren't they, bordering as they always did on a species of well-disguised infomercials, and, uh, Ker guesses it was just possible this one was taped like four years ago, twenty-four hours before he stepped into The Vinyl Fetish, or maybe seventy-two, or maybe three months, which isn't the point, is it, but nonetheless ... maybe it represents just one of those little secrets lovers keep from each other, or ... just unexplored psychological territory that would under the right circumstances become totally mappable.

Unless, it goes without saying, it *wasn't* Syndi, but one of those look-alikes you see all the time on the streets around town who you could *swear* was like Ellen DeGeneres or that woman from *Friends* or something, except she wasn't.

277. FLASH EMOTION

With one hand Ker tips back the Bud for a long mind-clearing swig and with the other flips channels in reverse, descending the decision tree, trying to relocate that show ... only, of course, that's never the way things work, which is the way things always work.

This horrendous green snot bubble balloons out some pig-snouted kid's left nostril and the well-dressed woman across from her at the nice L.A. restaurant begins spontaneously kecking.

Click.

A woman with stelliform shoe-polish black hair's head derricks up and down in a man's naked lap.

Click.

Prosthetic surgery is painful, but it can powerfully renew our sense of in-volvement in the world. It's all a question of where you locate the information interface: how much you can stand to lop off, or just how far back you're willing to

Click.

A reddish-brown male *Cimex lectularius* (bedbug to you and me) in ghastly close-up stabs its beak into a female's abdomen, preparing to re-lease its sperm into her wound and hence bloodstream.

Click.

Tribal drums and primitive wails blossom. Colors whirl. Black men in grass skirts and jangling brass earrings, bracelets, and necklaces dance wildly around a bonfire, shaking spears, lifting knees, hooting and jab-bering at night spirits. Earlobes hanging to jawbones. Scars funneling cheeks. Ker believes they're real, but also feels there's an equal chance he's just watching a rerun of *Gilligan's Island*.

They leap and caper around a naked body tied to the ground, ready for sacrifice. Arms stretched out to the sides. Legs wide apart. The face alert, familiar ... very familiar.

Hey, wait a second.

404. DUCK & COVER
What you gone do about it? the barrel-chested man in the black cowboy hat asks.

This! the barrel-chested man in the white cowboy hat shouts, flipping an oily blue revolver into view.

Good lord God, *no*! the mother in the white cowboy hat cries, trying to stand.

The barrel-chested man in the black cowboy hat tries to duck and cover. But it's too late. The barrel-chested man in the white cowboy hat fires. China crashes. Crystal splinters. A chair cracks against the floor.

Ugggh! the mother in the white cowboy hat cries, apparently fatally wounded.

380. AS A SOAP OPERA
It is also worth mentioning that although egg consumption in the United States is one-half of what it was in 1945, there has not been a comparable decline in heart disease. Moreover, although the American Heart Association deems eggs hazardous, a diet without them can be equally hazardous. Not only do eggs have the most perfect protein components of any food, but they al

532. DUCK & COVER
A glistening black Porsche sizzes through what looks like downtown Dallas or maybe it's downtown Miami or L.A. late at night, screeching around corners, turboing through intersections. A Corvette jets down avenue after avenue, low slung, white, locked in overdrive. Scattered gunfire. Because of the rapid jump cuts, it's not completely clear who's chasing who. Close-up of Rex Rory behind the wheel of one of the cars, perspiration sparkling on his face, fury in his eyes, hatred in the corners of his mouth ... and

most likely, given the context, not playing the flamboyant resident (though this obviously is open to debate and readjustment through viewing time), followed by the close-up of that barrel-chested man in the black cowboy hat from that other show, maybe, sweat sparkling on his face, eyes wide with fear, nose now broken and swelling, who isn't, in fact, Ker is almost sure, the guy from the other show, though it's possible he is, in which case next week's episode is playing simultaneously with this week's, only on a different channel, or maybe the syndicated iteration (whose name is on the tip of Ker's tongue) from let's say two seasons ago is cycling simultaneously with the so-far-non-syndicated version, only on an et cetera. Ker in any case has the distinct impression he's missed too many pieces of the plot to understand very much. An excess of lines have been spoken without him there to hear. He might as well give up. Plus in all honesty he may have seen this one before ... until, that is, the wedge-shaped spaceship appears, a glowing green delta above the city, and simply tremendous, as in the size of a hovering battleship, no, larger, and it's busy shooting some sort of photon-torpedo-looking jobs at *both* cars, only the aliens inside are really bad aims and keep nuking wads of unsuspecting tourists who have no right to be standing on street corners at this time of night in this kind of sketchy neighborhood anyway. Until, that is, the camera zips inside said ship, and Ker sees the two standard-issue cute human kids at the control panels, maybe twelve or thirteen years old, all agitated, trying to fly this thing and clearly pushing the wrong buttons by accident, and it dawns on Ker the whole business is really a comedy, the kids having crept aboard said craft probably built by dad in like Arizona or something and bumped the throttle without knowing it and now are on some kind of goofy joyride, ha ha ... unless, natch, Ker thinks, they aren't kids at all, but scary kids-appearing aliens, maybe pod-kids, and this ducks-in-a-barrel thing is their idea of a good time, a 3-D video game, and maybe they aren't on earth at all, but their home planet, a-and this is simply their playground out back or in their cellar, a-and the guys in the cars and all the bystanders have been unknowingly kidnapped and transported here while they slept, a-and they still believe they're in Dallas or Miami or L.A., which from their perspective is being invaded, in which case it's really a horror film that's über-intelligently conceived, though Ker kind of doubts it, but decides to go along with that theory, since it'll if nothing else make viewing more palatable. Until one of the kids or pod-kids or whatever lifts a can of something apparently called a Zerp Cola and takes a chug followed by a wide satisfied smile, and the announcer, this French guy who sounds like he's on amphetamines, says something lickety-split that Ker can't quite catch, though he once back-packed through France for two weeks, and in college took two years of the stuff, and Ker realizes he's been inhabiting a commercial masquerading as a horror film masquerading as a comedy masquerading as an action adventure masquerading as a soap opera and

176. NEWS: BREAK
A blueblack fly alights on the eyebrow of a young black boy whose facial skin has shrunk and withered like

299. THE GREAT WHEEL SPINS
The great wheel spins, brilliant light fizzling. The audience shouts. The game show host smiles. Bertha Marcella, fifty-eight, from What Cheer, Iowa, with a son in the Marines, jumps up and down, fat chugging, and claps her tiny hands in glee.

Then a shadow crosses her face.

She feels the pang, the elephant sitting on her chest, the lightening in her left arm. Her face muscles go slack. Her hands drop to her sides. Her eyes look up at the ceiling in disbelief. Bertha opens her mouth, sticks out her tongue, and topples over backwards.

She is wearing, Ker notices, a Timex on her left wrist.

231. THE DISCOVERY: CHANNEL
A cartoon dust cloud churns across the cartoon desert under a cartoon sky eerily pink instead of blue. It's Wile E. Coyote. He's wearing a pair of Acme rocket boots and the Roadrunner is doing that thing the Roadrunner always does, just kind of gliding nonchalantly along on those whirring legs of his … cool, calm, dum-de-dum, with even this like semi-reptilian smirk carved into his beak.

Ker expects those rocket boots to blow up any second. Or, you know, a huge rock or cactus to zoom up out of the desertscape and slam the poor carnivore so hard he can't stop vibrating for the remainder of the episode. O-or maybe some other gadget he tried to use earlier in the skit (an anvil, say, or an Acme ICBM, or a turbo-powered car right out of the Jetsons' garage) to appear and burn his sorry ass to a crisp cinder ... since, as Ker and every other philosophy major who's ever watched this show knows, Wile E. is none other than the animational embodiment of Camus's Sisyphus, and the Roadrunner his boulder, and the desert his hill, and the poor guy is just never going to win, it's so obvious it hurts. Wile E. is going to fall, explode, leap faithless into oblivion, squish, become existential flypaper for every bit of bad karma the uncaring universe can dish out. That's the given. That's how the show rolls. But his dignity (oh, yeah, have no doubt about it, folks: that's *dignity* you're watching there) arises from the fact that he *knows* this and just keeps going anyway, fuck the degenerates at Acme, you've got to *believe*, at least until you don't have to *believe*.

Except ... this time Ker thinks Wile E. is gaining ground. Yeah, he's actually closing the gap. There goes another ten yards, another five, and he's stretching both arms out in front of him, sort of leaning into the momentum as the exact same background cycles over and over again behind him, and the Roadrunner is actually looking over its shoulder now, a little nervous, that frozen smirk beginning to melt, and Wile E. reaches down to the control panel on his belt and hits OVERDRIVE.

Zooooooooooom!

A-and, *wham*, he's got him!

Wile E. grabs the Roadrunner by the neck with one hand and turns off his rocket boots with the other and there they are, huffing in this silent desert dance, orange sun setting behind them.

Only ... hey ... what's that? They ... they ... *embrace*! Yeah, that's what they do. A-and if the truth be known there's nothing even remotely female about that big bird, if you know what I mean, and ... a-and ...

The Roadrunner slips Wile E. his tongue, and Wile E. reciprocates, a-and pretty soon it sort of inches up on Ker that the Roadrunner's just been playing hard to get all this time ... yeah, that's it, the whole thing's been one big come-on ... and now what you've got yourself here are two really randy cartoon characters, a-and old Wile E.'s getting down on his paws and knees ... a-and the Roadrunner's kind of shuffling up behind him ...

169. THE LOVEBOAT

Nona Nova, hospital nurse, stares forlornly at herself in the mirror, unzips her uniform, reveals her tight belly, bronze skin, pert breasts barely hidden under lacy bra. She runs warm water in the sink. Splashes her face. Reaches for a handful of paper towels. When she looks in the mirror again another head floats behind hers: Rex Rory, flamboyant resident.

Nona cracks a smile.

Rex steps into the women's restroom and shuts the door behind him, flashes her a flawless grin. They embrace.

Oh god, how I've missed you! Nona murmurs into his ear.

Yes! he whispers. *Yes!*

They kiss. She reaches for his belt. He reaches for her breasts. Her belly. For the astonishing curve of her spine.

Hey, wait a second, he says, feeling that weird bulge in her panties. What's this?

251. A PRICK

The male platypus possesses a hollow claw, or spur, on each hind leg. The spurs are connected with poison glands. The platypus pricks and poisons its enemies when it feels threatened.

382. PRIME: TIME: LIVE

There is no white bouquet of chute, slowing of momentum, sound save the whipping of wind far above the tiny red, white, and blue dot.

You watch him flap his arms.

You watch him kick his legs.

You watch him speeding down, faster and faster. Hurtling straight for the jagged rocks and shallow river below. The strong current. The icy water. The twisted bodies of those who tried and failed be

203. NEWS: BREAK: VANISHING POINT

No human female could physically endure actual embodiment in Barbie's ultra-slim proportions. Her bones would be too thin and brittle, the force of gravity too strong. Not to mention the unbearable agony of elongating, emaciating, and eviscerating her

188. ADDRESS AT VISION 31

Uh-oh, Kerwin says, glancing down at the last bite of his sandwich pinched between thumb and forefinger. He isn't feeling so hot all of a sudden. His stomach's queasy and his head's ... it's kind of like when you have the flu and the rest of the world looks to you like you're squinting at it through a layer of Saran Wrap.

He starts giving some serious thought to that mayonnaise, puts the last bite on the end-table next to his beanbag chair. Plus he hasn't been paying attention to the time and realizes the light in the room has changed for the unmistakably more somber, taken on resolutely late-afternoon hues, unless obviously the sky has clouded up, in which case it could still be morning ... only he senses Syndi should be here by now. The apartment should be aware of her presence. He should be listening to her tell him about her day as she concocts dinner in the kitchen.

107. VINYL FETISH

Mildred Openheimer, sixty-three, from Onaway, Idaho, with a son in the Air Force, opens her mouth, sticks out her tongue, and topples backwards. She hits the floor like a whale dropped from a 747.

Just at the moment the wheel stops spinning, its arrow pointing to JACKPOT. Sirens shriek. Buzzers trill. Alarms rattle to life. The game show host, Sam Slant, close-cropped graying beard and slicked-back hair, still smiling, looks down at Mildred, up at the camera, over at the other contestants.

Um, he says.

Which leads Ker to assume he's watching a game show until the two detectives in black, one short and one tall, one chubby and one the opposite, walk out on stage and it becomes clear this is the old game-show-within-a-police-show trope, at which instant Ker realizes Mildred is being played by Sandi Slam, the same young actress who plays Nona Nova, only here she's all decked out in layers of foam to make her look huge and aged, which impresses Ker a lot, from a professional point of view, but not as much as the explanation that the short chubby detective with a head shaped vaguely like an anvil delivers, hardly moving his lips, as paramedics begin to work on poor Mildred whose mouth is opening and closing like a pithed frog's.

Mildred Openheimer, unhappily married to one Marvin Openheimer, and unhappily mothered to Murray, Mini, and Mimmi Openheimer, and feeling really alone way out there in Onaway, Idaho, it turns out from the detectives' explanation, became involved with the Internet as a way to meet people. She joined a number of chat groups. One of them, which she thought had to do with discussing old-time records, was called The Vinyl Fetish and was frequented by all manner of S&M types, one of whom went by the moniker Slowhand.

Mildred fell through the looking glass into a world she never knew possible, and she liked what she found there. So before long she took on the handle Black Widow, having little appellative imagination at her disposal, and off she went.

At first Mildred and Slowhand gabbed nightly online while Marvin stared at the tube just a couple of feet away, spinning all manner of increasingly torqued fantasies to basically pass the time … except then they gradually elided into email correspondence, where suffice it to say the words *penis rings* and *nice gradual strangulation* came up a whole bunch more frequently than in what you might conceptualize as conventional day-to-day friendly exchanges.

One morning a month ago Mildred waited for Marvin and the kids to leave for work and school, respectively, packed a suitcase, and, without even scribbling a goodbye note, vamoosed, traveling via train to L.A. where Slowhand (aka one Ralph Schnorz) was waiting.

They met at a hotel where Schnorz employed some of the ideas on Mildred they'd been discussing digitally, then went downtown where they got her on this game show, The Great Wheel Spins, and, seconds before she took the stage, fed her three prophylactics packed with heroin, each sporting a hairline tear, which ruptured the eyeblink she began jumping up and down, releasing enough diacetylmorphine into her system to kill something like eighteen elephants, executing the sadomasochistic double-suicide pact they'd been weaving for almost a year.

Hic, hic, hic, Sam Slant, game-show host, says, beginning to gag. Hic, hic, hic.

He reaches up and with a flourish yanks off his beard and toupee, revealing, yep, the bald-headed pock-marked features of none other than

Ralph Schnorz, sadomasochistic killer, who has himself just bitten down on a cyanide capsule he bought on a recent trip to Tijuana, but not before ripping away his clip-on tie, popping the buttons down the front of his white Armani shirt, and dipping inside for one more yank on the biggest tit clamps you've ever seen, more like something you'd find on a work-table in a hobby shop than anything you'd ever expect to find on your average

199. AS A SOAP OPERA

Rex Rory, flamboyant resident, slaps her. Punches her on the shoulders. Nona Nova, hospital nurse, laughs at his foolish lopsided smacks.

You no good bitch! he yells. You think I'm just another one of your toys you can play with and throw away? You think you can sleep with me and turn round and sleep with my sister, my own *sister*, Rita Rory, without a thought? Well, you're gonna pay for this! You're gonna wished you never laid eyes on me!

Nona Nova flashes him one of her flawless patented grins until Rex flips an oily blue revolver into view.

313. REVOLVER

And so, Paul McCartney says, interviewing (if Ker's not mistaken) Marshall McLuhan on some minimalist powder-blue set, the thing is, aren't we really talking about an ideological shift in the social dominant?

Um, right, McLuhan says, running a nervous hand across his salt-and-pepper hair, obviously surprised to find himself talking to a rock legend. Because, um, well, all media, from the phonetic alphabet to the computer, are extensions of man that cause deep and lasting changes in him and transform his environment. Such an extension is an intensification, an amplification of an organ, sense or function, and whenever it takes place, the central nervous system appears to institute a self-protective *numbing* of the affected area ...

Insulates and anesthetizes it from conscious awareness?

A process rather like that which occurs to the body under shock or stress conditions, or to the mind in line with the Freudian concept of repression. Right.

So what you're saying, really, is that multiple subjectivities can't articulate their circumscribed reality—to employ a perhaps-outdated social construct—can they, until they've moved beyond that positional matrix?

McLuhan shoots McCartney a half-lidded suspicious glance.

The … um … right … Most people cling to what I call the rearview-mirror view of their world. I mean, because of the invisibility of any environment during the period of its innovation, man is only consciously aware of the environment that has *preceded* it. In other words, an environment becomes fully visible only when it has been superseded by a new environment. Thus we're always one step behind in our perception of the world.

So what you're suggesting is the ideological imperative becomes re-contextualized only through a spacio-temporal reconfiguration?

I … hey, who are you?

Paul, dude.

No. I'm serious. Who are you … *really*?

I'm, em, Paul. The Beatles and all?

You're not. Paul doesn't talk like that. No way.

There's always more to Paul than meets the eye.

Stop it. You're scaring me.

Ever wondered why he never shows any signs of aging, for example?

Stop.

Oh, sure, a little gray hair like five years ago, and then … poof … nothing.

I'm covering my ears and whistling to myself here.

I've got two words for you.

I see your mouth moving but I refuse to listen.

Two words.

268. NATURE IS NOT NICE

How many teenagers are left? First four. Then three. Then two. Now only one: the most beautiful. Fair angel. Eighteen and mostly naked. Lace panties and bra. Bespattered with mud. Wet blond hair matted to face. Trickles of water and tears zigging down her cheeks. Trapped in the barn of the desolate farm. Stalked by Zodiac Killer, homicidal maniac. Violent rainstorm. In each enormous lightning flash a huge shadow looms closer. She screams. She crawls. She stands. She sits, paralyzed by mortality.

Zodiac Killer wields a pitchfork in one hand and a whirring chainsaw in the other. He towers over her, laughing.

The teen must learn how to lose gracefully.

Because, in her back pocket, she's carrying a nearly used-up tube of gash-red lipstick and, if she's not murdered right this second, Zodiac Killer knows, she will drive to the coast two months hence to quietly reflect upon her past and contemplate her future options (a major in business at Slippery Rock Community College? a major in education at Fairleigh Dickinson?) and that tube will accidentally work its way out of her back pocket and pop onto the sand where the cute little French boy who starred in that commercial for Zerp will, vacationing on Coney Island with his parents during his first holiday to the U.S. (in celebration of his ascending career), pick it up forty-one days later and chuck it as far as he can into the Atlantic Ocean on a reflexive whim.

Little will he understand as he does so that that tube will comprise the last piece of human shit thrown into the ocean before all the human shit thrown into the ocean over all the millennia of human shit-in-the-ocean-throwing finally reaches some critical mass, generating a molecular flashpoint where all the nascent waste-nanites flushed down secret-lab toilets over the last decade off the coast of New Jersey will merge with various contraceptives, industrial sludge, artificial fruit juices for kids, and cheap metals (including that tube of gash-red lipstick) to become in one shocking burst sentient, nor that that mess's first thought will concern itself with destroying the ignorant lower life forms hogging all the good dry space on the planet, meaning mostly humanoids, and hence launching a massive assault on the race, first by sneaking up on and at-tacking unsuspecting swimmers, then surfers, small-boaters, large-ship-pers, and, on one momentous day in August, by loosing a blitzkrieg on Tokyo, New York, and London, resulting within fewer than four months in the earth having been turned into a big ball of very intelligent gray nano-goo.

205. PRIME: TIME: LIVE
Bad would have to be an understatement for how Ker feels. He thinks one word over and over: *bathroom*. He shakily rises to propel himself posthaste down the hall … which is when the pounding at the front door commences.

130. HE DO THE POLICE IN DIFFERENT VOICES
Thomas Stearns Eliot, born in St. Louis on September 26, 1888, was one of the greatest

166. THE GREAT WHEEL SPINS
A car burns out of control. Upside down. A bus on top of it. Orange and black fireball. But whose car? Where? Under what circumstances? Who's inside?

524. LOVEBOAT
It's too late. The barrel-chested man in the black cowboy hat shoots. China crashes. Crystal splinters. A chair cracks against the floor. But the mother in the white cowboy hat shoots first. With her tommy gun. The barrel-chested man in the white cowboy hat cries out, astounded, chest riddled with bullets. He slumps to his knees.

Mama … he says, surprised.

His mother laughs, embraces the barrel-chested man in the black cowboy hat, united with her lover at last.

299. NATURE IS NOT NICE
Jogging down the hall, Ker feels something expand in his bowels like a film of a blossoming black carnation on fast-forward. The pounding at the front door grows louder, more insistent. He groans, stops, turns, sort of shuffle-hops a couple of paces toward the living room, thinks better of it, turns, trots toward the bathroom, halts when the pounding detonates into banging, begins worrying about Syndi again (it simply *has* to be time for her to get home), halts, cradles his belly like a pregnant woman, turns, shuffle-hops towards the front door, earnestly contemplates embarrassing himself in front of a stranger, concludes this couldn't be Syndi,

she wouldn't pound like that, turns, trots toward the bathroom, halts when he realizes she wouldn't pound like that *unless it was an emergency*, turns, shuffle-hops toward the front door, undoes the two bolts and chain and lock, cracks it open, and . . . *BLAM*!!!

301. NATURE IS NOT NICE

In explodes Zodiac Killer, and, fuck, is he *big* . . . seven feet tall if an inch, and somehow that ski mask makes him look only that much bigger, and the huge Bowie knife, too, it almost goes without saying, which he's currently resting against Ker's throat, having with his forearm pinned him to the wall, and he's *smiling*.

It strikes Ker he's never thought about Zodiac Killer's breath before, but now comprehends it has the same moisture and fecal reek as the air maybe two inches above a garbage dump on the outskirts of São Paulo on a hot summer afternoon.

Ker shuts his eyes as his bowels round the homestretch toward a pure plasma state.

Zodiac Killer chortles.

Your girlfriend, he whispers . . . she *liked* it, is the thing. Some don't. She asked for more. Know what she said before I hoisted her off the floor with the noose? Before she shat herself and died? *Do me harder, sweetmeat. Do me* . . . Hic-hic-hic. Hic-hic-hic.

Ker opens his eyes.

A fairly large rivulet of blood running out of Zodiac Killer's right nostril is the first thing he sees. Next he catches sight of that fire poker jutting out of the homicidal maniac's head like some weird TV antenna. And next he understands, very briefly, that, despite the guy's breath, he really takes very good care of his teeth.

Because those teeth are all on display right now as Zodiac Killer begins to squeak and rotate around simultaneously, at which point Ker sort of slides down the wall and notices . . . he's somehow wearing *lace panties and a bra*. How the hell did *that* happen? A-and his own pert teenage breasts fascinate him so much he can't help lifting a palm to cup one a-and cop a quick feel, only . . . *whump* . . . the chair shatters across Zodiac Killer's back . . . and there . . . above and left . . . who *is* that?

None other than the strikingly handsome nineteen-year-old baby-faced boy, Keane or Keir or Kendall or Kipp or Kyle, whom Zodiac Killer shishkebabed earlier in the made-for-TV movie with another (and, in this case, barbed) red-hot fire poker ... a-and yet ... a-and yet . . . he's *walking* . . . Keane or Keir or Kendall or Kilian or Kyle's inching along, poker still sticking through his chest, not quite dead yet, still time for one last act of really impressive selfless heroism ... flawless teeth in *his* grin, too, a-and the drop-dead gorgeous guy raises two fingers to his forehead in a flip salute to posterity, gingerly releases an oily blue revolver from his back pocket, takes aim.

Yippie-kay-eh, motherfucker, he says, and pulls the trigger.

But, unfortunately, misses.

230. HE DO THE POLICE IN DIFFERENT VOICES

Rex Rory, flamboyant resident, releases an oily blue revolver from his back pocket, takes aim, and shoots Nona Nova, hospital nurse, once, just below her pert twentysomething left breast, yet not before Nona Nova releases an oily blue revolver from her ... where, exactly? ... the logistics have somehow escaped Ker ... and shoots him point blank in the groin. Twice. They fall to their respective knees.

Strumpet! he shouts, blood bubbling from his lips.

Reprobate cuckold! she shouts, clutching her throat for no particular reason Ker can discern.

287. ADDRESS AT VISION 31

The great wheel spins. The audience shouts insanely. The game show host smiles with pure confidence. Madge Moertel, fifty-seven, from Whitewater, Wisconsin, with a son in Attica, jumps up and down, fat chugging, and claps her tiny hands in glee. The wheel spits fire. The wheel spits flame. Lights flash like lightning, and ... slowly ... the wheel clicks to a halt, its arrow pointing to JACKPOT. Sirens shriek. Buzzers trill. Alarms rattle. And Madge Moertel leaps into the air like an African chieftain. Bounds into the arms of the host. Her daughter rockets out of the audience and slaps onto the bi-hominidal cluster. Madge Moertel wins a dream vacation to Haiti. Madge Moertel wins a year's supply of cat food for her dog. Madge

Moertel's face sprouts a flower, her fingers sprout diamonds, her eyes roll up under her lids and she ignites. All around her people duck and cover.

335. WHITE QUEEN: BODILESSNESS: DARK

Which is when the ants come. Ker lying flat on his back in his lace bra and panties beside his beanbag chair in the living room, unable to move so much as an eyelid, watching the ceiling swarm with them. In fact, it seems as if the ceiling doesn't even really exist anymore, that it's been in-sectivally devoured, that the black ants have somehow *become* the ceiling through the act of ingesting it, a vibrant black undulating mass … which would have been unpleasant in itself, but the ants? They aren't just *above* his head. They're *inside* his head, too.

Ker can feel them skittering over the bones that comprise his skull where all that facial and cranial skin of his used to hang. Feel them seethe in place of his tongue. Rush through his sinuses, over the backs of his eye-balls, migrate up his otic canals, nibble through his ear drums, make burger of his hammers and anvils and stirrups and cochleae, single-file down his Eustachian tubes, blast up his auditory nerves in a screech of B-film noise.

They assemble ant ranches in the creases of his cerebral cortex and the queen, gloopy and gnarled as a big white turd, excavates his cerebellum and begins birthing thousands of larval rice-eggs, which is awful, yes, but not as awful as when her troops force their way down Ker's esophagus and branch out into his lungs, ripping their way through mealy tissue, planting hundreds of larvae in some semi-mucusy lung sacs, meaning Ker begins to cough, feeling like he can't catch his breath, till he forgets about that slight discomfort because they've also made their way into his heart, it feels like, though maybe it's just the lower reaches of his trachea, at which point he lurches into a full-blown grand-mal seizure, or what from his perspec-tive feels like a full-blown grand-mal seizure, but can't be, in point of fact, since he still retains a semblance of consciousness.

Except what *really* scares him is when they get into his stomach, which about now feels like he's just gargled with a bottle of Sani-Flush, this mass of damnation irrupting into volcanic steam clouds when it hits meaty bot-tom and pretty much vaporizing his gall bladder and liver, and you don't even want to ask about his bile duct or poor little fried knot of duodenum, before full-speeding into his intestines, both large and small, causing him instantaneously to go liquid, simultaneously projectile vomiting blood-ants from his mouth, on the one hand, and spewing them in a hot muddy red jet from his anus, on the other, before what *really* spooks him happens, which is that he next just sort of goes—what's the word?—supernova.

One second he's there and the next he detonates, ka-*blam!*, covering the ceiling, which has become ants, and the walls, which have become ants, and the floors, which have become ants, with ants and more ants and chunks of organs and flaps of skin and wads of hair, *his* organs and skin and hair, only he maintains a certain essential third-party awareness throughout all this, somehow, which, natch, shakes him, but not as much as when those organ chunks and skin flaps and hair wads that used to be Kerwin Penumbro sprout compound eyes and six legs each and antennae and almost imperceptibly small stingers on their asses a-and start tooling away, single-file, a miniature battalion of buggish body parts marching in different directions, merging with the ant soup all around them, the ant sea, a-and Ker lies there in his lace bra and panties, terrified, flat on his back, just watching his shredded selves disappear into the deep, into the dark, into that huge black nidus of bloodcurdling selflessness …

185. THE DISCOVERY: CHANNEL
Ker? Syndi asks tentatively, poking her head through the apartment door. Ker? That you? Hey, happy birthday, lover! … Hey … and but … uh, what's all this?

200. THE LOVEBOAT
How many teenagers are left? First four. Then three. Then two. Now only one: the most beautiful. Fair angel. Eighteen and mostly naked. Lace panties and over-large Sick Poppies t-shirt of this black woodcut of this female bedbug stabbing its beak into this male bedbug's abdomen, preparing to release its fertilized eggs into his wound and bloodstream. Wire-rimmed glasses bespattered with mud. Wet ponytail come undone. Honey hair matted to face.

It's … hey … it's *Syndi*! Ker'd recognize her anywhere. She's trapped in the barn of the desolate farm, stalked by Zodiac Killer, homicidal maniac, violent rainstorm crashing outside. In each enormous lightning flash a huge shadow looms closer. She screams. She crawls. She stands. She sits, paralyzed by mortality, preparing to learn how to lose gracefully.

Zodiac Killer wields a pitchfork in one hand (Timex on wrist, you can't miss the product placement), a whirring chainsaw in the other. He towers over her, laughing … a-and then, totally unexpectedly, he chucks his pitchfork left, chainsaw right. Syndi cringes. The chainsaw sputters and dies.

Zodiac Killer reaches up, grabs hold of his ski mask, and tugs. Beneath the mask is … is … weh-hell … it's *Ker*! Syndi looks up, disbelieving at first, then a grin spreads across her sweet countenance. She stands, enters his parted arms.

Ker, she says, Ker …

It's okay, babe, says Ker, we made it.

They embrace. They kiss. On the lips. Syndi reaches for his belt. Ker reaches for her pert teenage breasts. Her firm belly. For the astonishing curve of her

267. IMMORTALITY: STEALTH

The phone rings. Ker's eyes pop open. He's been sleeping. The room's dark except for the blue photonic haze from the Stealth's screen. What time is it? He reaches for his cellphone on the floor beside him.

Myellow?

Mr. Penumbro?

Um, yeah? he says, blinking himself awake.

Mr. Penumbro, this is the Seattle Police Department. You've been listed as next of kin on Syndi Shogunn's living will. Can you get down to the hospital right away?

164. DELTA: ART ALLUSION: SWEEPS

Claude, Claude's father Clyde, man with the knowing smile, says to the cute little French boy from the commercial as he steps off the wedge-shaped spaceship, all happy endings, you know I love you.

I love you too, dad, Claude says.

They grin. They embrace. They kiss. On the lips. Claude reaches for Clyde's belt. Clyde reaches for Claude's breasts. His belly. For the astonishing

130. UNCLE BUDDY'S PHANTOM FUNHOUSE
Man thus becomes the sex organs of the machine world just as the bee is of the plant world, permitting it to reproduce and constantly evolve to higher forms …

141. AS SEEN ON TV
The phone rings. Ker's eyes pop open. He's been sleeping. The room's dark except for the blue photonic haze from the Stealth's screen. What time is it? He reaches over for his cellphone on the couch beside him.

Myellow?

Ker?

Um, yeah? he says, blinking himself awake.

Ker, it's me.

Syndi?

I'm running a little late. Hey, you okay? You sound a little … I don't know.

277. SHE DO THE POLICE IN DIFFERENT VOICES
I see a young woman, says psychic healer Abbey Rode, whose hair reminds Ker of a red rubber wig. Abbey has that slack-muscled serious-yet-utterly-accepting face only drugged children and talk-show psychic healers have. Her eyes are closed in concentration.

Blond hair, she says. Wire-rimmed glasses. She's on a farm, an isolated farm, a-and she will die tonight.

309. PLAY: SIN
Zodiac Killer wields a pitchfork in one hand, a whirring chainsaw in the other. He towers over her, laughing. Syndi cringes. The chainsaw flies down.

But misses.

Syndi leaps up, head-butting him in the groin. He folds in pain. She yanks the pitchfork from his grip and drives it home, smack into the middle of his forehead.

Blood burbles from his lips and he does that death-shudder thing peo-ple in low-budget made-for-TV movies do.

Syndi yanks out the pitchfork, reaches down, grabs hold of his ski mask, and tugs. Beneath the mask is … is … weh-hell … it's *Ker*! Syndi stares, disbelieving, then a grin gradually spreads across her sweet countenance. She breaks into laughter.

About fucking time, she says.

491. RUBBER WIG: ART: CRIMES

A woman with stelliform shoe-polish black hair's head derricks up and down in a man's naked lap.

The camera pans back.

A pizza delivery man in khaki shirt is taking her from behind. Between his legs lies a second woman clearly wearing a cheap blond wig, lapping at the delivery man's privates. Ker can't get a good look at her, but even in that wig, from this angle, it looks just like … doesn't it?

217. ADDRESS AT VISION 31

The rock'n'roll star hangs under the ocean, ultramarine, pine green, indigo, gray, singing for his mate. Bubbles sizzle out of his mouth. He raises two fingers to his forehead in a flip salute to posterity, unaware of the great white shark speeding in behind him, flawless teeth in its grin.

214. SWEEPS: AS A SOAP OPERA: VANISHING POINT

Rex Rory, behind the wheel of one of the cars (though which is unclear), perspiration sparkling on his face, fury in his eyes, hatred at mouth corners, sticks his oily blue revolver out the window and squeezes off two shots. The glowing green delta over the city wobbles. Cut to the two children at the control panels, faces raided with terror, clutching each other and screaming. The ship ignites. A tremendous explosion spreads across the sky, an orange and black fireball.

Below people duck and cover, thinking they are saved from the terrible invaders, but are wrong, because a single germ from planet Zerp will sur-vive this nuclear blaze and float down to earth where more than a week later, landing on a fifty-dollar bill extended in the hand of one Mary

Christmas to pay Dick Smoker for the crack cocaine she desperately needs to feed her recent addiction in the wake of her dad's recent bizarre demise (fetish encasement, lack of breathing tubes).

That germ will be passed via said bill across the country, then across the Atlantic to Berlin, via the hands of a tourist named Gaye Powwers, where it will be exchanged for Euros, during which process the germ will fall on the floor, where it will wait six more months, till a little snot-nosed girl whose name isn't really important will deliberately drop a wad of Bazooka bubble-gum on it, which gum a Pekingese named Fopstein will later that day eat, passing the germ through his system unscathed while on a train bound for Prague, in which city he will deposit said germ by means of a well-formed pile of shit on his master's nice white rug at three in the a.m., and where his master's son, Fritz, distant ancestor of Franz Kafka's bastard child, at that stage where he has to taste everything, will pick it up and actually take a bite first thing next morning, bringing the germ to consciousness as it hits those special stomach acids that spell H-U-M-A-N, at which point said germ will begin to multiply, releasing a plague that will cause people to see what happened to them four seconds ago, instead of what's happening to them now, which will within the course of six years kill off the entire population of the planet by means of various ghastly accidents (car crashes, elevator mishaps, defenestration), paving the way for the next species to dominate the earth ... not the cockroach, as it is usually assumed, but the feathery-antennaed moth which, to this moment, had just been minding its own business, biding its time.

170. NATURE IS NOT NICE
Wile E. Coyote rises with great dignity, wipes the drop of whitish foam from his bottom with a handkerchief he gingerly produces ... from where, exactly? ... and hobbles toward the sunset as the Roadrunner, lounging by a boulder, rests his left heel on his right knee, lights a cigarette, and begins to thought-bubble dream of Marshall McLuhan in lace bra and panties.

213. THE DISCOVERY: CHANNEL
You wait one one-thousand, two one-thousand, three, trying to convince yourself this can't be happening.

He plummets like a starfish.

There is no white bouquet of chute, no slowing of momentum, no sound save the whipping of wind far above the tiny red, white, and blue dot.

You watch him flap his arms and kick his legs.

You watch him speeding down, faster and faster ... shooting down ... hurtling straight for the jagged rocks and shallow river threading below.

The strong current.

The icy water.

The twisted bodies of those who tried and failed before him.

Seventy feet to go ... forty ... twenty ... a–and then: *whoosh*!

A–and then: *ahhhhh*!

A–and then and then and then: he pulls the backup cord and a beautiful orange and black hang glider unfolds from his parachute pouch like wings. He skims the whitewater, zips over the jagged rocks, ascends above the pine trees in a miraculous arc, higher and higher, a fair angel.

As he swoops up toward you, you see his face ... his familiar face ... his very familiar face. Beneath the lightening bolts on his helmet you make out Ker's features, those flawless teeth in his grin.

He zooms closer, raises two fingers to his forehead in a flip salute to posterity, and, when you blink again, he's ... gone.

FROM

Hideous Beauties

(2003)

Sixteen Jackies

NO, I DON'T REMEMBER SMILING. Of course, I don't remember not smiling, either. I honestly don't remember much of anything about that day. I mean, there was that rush of sun across my face as Jack and I stepped off the plane. I remember that. And I remember how I tried to stay very close to him as we moved down the line of people with welcome banners crowding us at Love Field. Only I kept getting pushed away from him by admirers trying to shake his hand. There was the terrible heat softening the leather in the limo, I remember, and John and Nellie looking across at us from the jump seat, and Jack sitting to my right. He waved like a hero returning from the War as we rolled into the tunnel toward the center of town and I remember thinking *Maybe it will be slightly cooler in there*, and then the white flicker of realities changing as we came out the other side, the way he turned into a marionette whose strings someone had cut. He didn't make a sound. There was what seemed like the backfire from a motorcycle, *pop*, followed by another *pop*, and his left hand flew up, and he assumed this quizzical expression for a moment, and then he put his other hand to his forehead and turned into a marionette and fell sideways into my lap.

Next I was scrambling across the black trunk burning with sunshine, reflexively trying, I suspect, to collect pieces of him so that I could put him back together again, and people were I think grabbing at me, and the next thing I knew I was drifting in the middle of a gray confusion. I remember saying *I love you, Jack, I love you*, although, of course, I didn't. Love him, that is. Not any more. I hadn't loved him for years. How could I? Imagine all those women. It was intolerable.

And I remember—afterwards, that is, many days or perhaps even weeks afterwards—seeing news footage of all those events looping, all those other things that happened, all those other things I apparently did, except I don't actually remember doing them. It's the strangest thing. I don't remember myself doing the things I did, but I remember seeing the footage of me doing them.

You know how they say you're supposed to recall every single detail about critical instants in your life? What things smelled like? Each thing you touched?

It didn't work that way for me at all.

I mean, I don't even remember whether or not I smiled that day.

Actually, you probably remember more about those weeks than I do. That dazed look on my face as I stood next to Lyndon? The hearse drawn by those gorgeous horses down Pennsylvania Avenue? Little John holding my hand and then letting it fall away as he raised his own to salute his father's casket? You can't forget those things, can you? They'll always be there, like your fingerprints. At one point you may even have mapped your entire experience according to them. Many people did. Those pictures represent a powerful flinch in the biography of this country. Yet all I can summon up—besides what I just told you, that is, besides those few sense impressions—all I can summon up is that gray confusion that swallowed me the second I heard those backfires. It may have lasted hours. It may have lasted days. It felt like it lasted decades. Like a kind of—I don't quite know how to say it—a kind of existential suspension the color of seasickness.

I'm not very good with words. I'm sorry. I worked in publishing for years, if you can believe it, but truth is I only read manuscripts for the story line. The thing is this: when the confusion finally did lift it lifted very quickly. So quickly, in fact, that it felt a little like an exhaust fan had been turned on and had just sucked all the stuporous smoke right out of the stuporous-smoke-filled room called my brain. There I was, sitting by Jack's side in the limo as we rolled into that tunnel, wondering if I might find a minute's reprieve from the awful Texas heat, and next it was two or three in the morning, and I was back in the White House, and I didn't know what day it was. I was in my nightgown and I was simply standing there, staring at my bed. From what I can reconstruct, this must have been sometime during the transition period—before Lyndon and Lady Bird began moving in their things, before I had moved mine out completely—because I remember seeing packing boxes stacked everywhere, and I remember the clutter on my writing desk and across the top of my chest of draws. I remember clothes spilling from my open closet door, and, somehow larger than life, as if seen through some sort of magnifying lens, I remember seeing an overturned vial of baby-blue sleeping pills by an empty glass on the bedside table.

What I remember most, though, after stepping off the plane and feeling that rush of sunshine across my face, was seeing *myself* lying under the sheets. I know. It sounds crazy. Only there I was, standing in my nightgown in the middle of my bedroom at the White House, watching myself sleep.

This is embarrassing to admit, but my first thought was that it must be one of Jack's women. I used to find them all over the place. When I was redecorating the building, I'd open an office door or poke my head into a nook I didn't usually poke my head into and there one would be sprawled on a couch or rifling through desk draws for memorabilia. *The nerve of that bitch*, I remember thinking. Excuse me, but that's what I thought. *The nerve of that bitch, sleeping in my bed after all that's happened.* Then I realized it was a mistake. She wasn't another woman. She was me. There I was, lying on my back, my right arm stretched almost flush with my right side and my left hand turned palm upward beside my head on my pillow. It cocked at such an odd angle that it seemed to me to be a separate sleeping entity. My breathing was heavy and steady. I'd probably taken more of those sleeping pills than I should have. I suppose all I wanted to do was leave the inside of my head until that horrible confusion went away. But that isn't what made an impression on me. Not really. What made an impression on me was what a mess my hair was. I was struck, if you want to know the truth, by how mussed up it seemed and how unbeautiful I appeared. I hoped no one would walk in and see.

I had always suspected my jaw was too wide, of course. Who wouldn't have? And my nose was too ... *excessive*, I believe is the word, by a third. These facts hit me with the force of absolute truth that night. Only what troubled me even more profoundly was something I had never noticed before: my lower lip rested too near my chin. I had never considered this, and yet there was no avoiding the issue: my chin had begun to recede. Or perhaps it had always been like that and I had just failed to notice. I imagine this is what people mean when they say *encroaching middle age.* Even now, here, I shudder at the very thought of it.

I stood there for what I think amounted to a couple minutes, awake without warning in the middle of my room at the White House, watching myself sleep. I was both fascinated and alarmed. In an instinctive gesture, I reached up and pressed my cheek with two fingers, as one might do to the flank of a sleeping dog to make sure it's really sleeping and not dead or something, and, across the room, the oddest thing occurred. How to say it? Another one of me—yes, that's the word—another one of me *unfolded* itself from the unconscious version, like a flower from a bud. It sat up, and, gazing groggily straight ahead, scratched the back of its skull, threw its feet over the side of the bed, stood, and glided out of the room as if I—the one of me that felt most like me at the time, that is—as if I simply didn't exist within the same dimension it inhabited.

When I turned toward the bed again, I saw another version of myself unfolding from the sleeping one. It shrugged itself off the mattress and wafted through the room and out the door. The same thing happened another three, eight, maybe twelve or thirteen times. The fact is I lost count. Or perhaps I forgot to count. You can imagine, I'm sure. I mean, there I was—everywhere.

Not long after the last one had departed, the sleeping version of me opened its eyes and took drowsy inventory of the room. I recall the light was already beginning to blanch into dawn. Eventually my double stood, cracked her neck, and shuffled right past me toward the bathroom. I didn't follow. For some reason I had lost all interest in what she was going to do in there. Instead, I walked over to the bed, bent down, and patted the area where a different me had just lain. The pillow was still indented with my head, the sheets still warm. I climbed onto the mattress on all fours, curled onto my side, collapsed, and remained as unmoving as I knew how, trying to fill my mind with zero except the sound of my galloping pulse. Eventually a spongy sleep seeped through my limbs, and the next time I became aware of my surroundings it was already early afternoon and Lady Bird was gently shaking me the way she sometimes did those days, telling me it was time to get up, dear—she called me *dear*—because I had a meeting with the Secret Service in just over an hour, and the world came back to me in a smear of harsh light and noise.

A number of weeks passed. The funeral you probably remember better than I do took place, Lyndon appropriated the reigns of power with perhaps more gusto than I felt was strictly decorous, and the country gradually returned to its habitual cadences, although everyone seemed to agree that something special had been left behind forever. I found a cute little apartment in Manhattan with a lovely view of Central Park and began settling into my new life. As much as one can do in such circumstances, I mean—because, really, there's never very much alternative, is there. Anyway, I found it best to keep to myself. It felt—right, somehow. I wore sunglasses and a floppy hat when I left the building. I kept my head down. I decided there was very little point in answering the telephone. Every time it rang, I slipped it into a drawer in the cherry wood table on which it sat in the foyer and waited for the ringing to stop. After a few weeks, when the ringing didn't stop, I simply unplugged it. I unplugged the television and the radio, too, and stood quietly behind my front door, listening, when someone buzzed. Eventually whoever it was would give up and go away. I started to read romance novels. Romance novels and fashion magazines. And I discovered the pleasures of Fudge Fantasy ice cream. I began to contemplate having my chin done, too, but in the end decided against it. What was the point? Every night I would take a couple baby-blue sleeping pills with a vodka and tonic, and every day I would regain consciousness sometime past noon. Then I would slip on a pair of jeans and a ratty gray sweatshirt and a pair of red sneakers with white trim and stroll down the block to a nice café for a cup of black coffee and a pastry. On the way there I would stop by a newsstand run by a man with a fleshy pink knob instead of a left hand and pick up a paper. A different paper each day, depending on my mood. On the way home I would buy a pint of ice cream for lunch.

It was at that nice café on a cool, blue Sunday morning in April, over a French roast and *pain au chocolat*, that I saw the first mention of my name in one of those horrible tabloids. It was buried well below the middle fold. There was no photograph accompanying it. The font they used for the headline was discrete. Another day, and I might have overlooked it entirely.

As it happened, though, I paused in mid-sip, set my coffee cup in its saucer, and read. Done, I couldn't help leaning back in my chair and, well … smiling. Now *that* smile I remember. You see, the clown who had written the piece had gotten every last particular wrong. According to her I was living the good life in Martha's Vineyard. There were continual sightings of me at fabulous parties in Boston on the arm of some famous civil rights lawyer. And rumor had it I'd lost weight. A *lot* of weight. An *unhealthy* amount, in fact. An unnamed source claimed I had recently confessed to an eating disorder. A psychologist was quoted as saying such behaviors were ultimately all about control issues. *When I am driving*, I was purported to have told the unnamed source, *all I can think about is how I wish every car would just stay in a straight line in its own lane, and I can't stand it when all the switches on the light plates in the house aren't pointing in the same direction.*

It's remarkable what license some people will take with the truth. And there I was, sitting in that café on that cool, blue Sunday morning in April, weighing more than I ever had in my life. My knees had trouble touching, if you want to know, my thighs were so big. But, still, I had to smile. With a piece like that floating around out there, I didn't have a thing to worry about. I was free and clear. So I just sat there, this huge smile on my face, finishing my coffee and trying to imagine the future. In no time, I figured, people would stop bothering me. They'd think I had moved up north, so they wouldn't call me and they wouldn't ring the bell and they wouldn't make me stand silently on the other side of the door, waiting for them to leave.

And that's pretty much what I did. I mean, I paid my bill and strolled back to my apartment—stopping in a corner shop on the way to pick up a trial pint of Oreo Dream and the latest issue of *Cosmo*—and by seven o'clock that evening I had put the whole incident out of mind.

Which is where it stayed until a week later, when my name surged up at me again from another paper. Only this time we weren't talking tabloid. We were talking the real thing. And my name wasn't tucked away in some small font near the back below the middle fold. It shouted at me in bold blocky letters from the top of the daily gossip column. There I was sitting at that nice café, trying to enjoy my Viennese blend, and suddenly I was reading about myself. I wasn't living in Manhattan, it turned out, and I wasn't living in Boston. I was living in Miami in a posh enclave right on the waterfront. My weight was down, thank goodness, my health good. But I had undergone a botched attempt at a facelift that had left me permanently scarred, so I had to wear a veil whenever I went out into public, and a rusty chain of financial setbacks had left me on the brink of bankruptcy.

Well, you simply can't imagine how distraught I was. Unexpectedly coming across a story about yourself like that is like unexpectedly coming across a tombstone with your name on it and realizing the birth date engraved on it matches yours perfectly. That horrid column unnerved me so much I couldn't concentrate on anything for the rest of that day. I put my pint of ice cream in the oven, a freshly toasted bagel in the dishwasher. An extra sleeping pill and a vodka and tonic that night accomplished nothing except to make me both sluggish *and* agitated. The next afternoon, just when my mind had taken a stab at recomposing itself, I came across the third mention. I was back at the café, this time picking at a large buttery croissant, when I found myself reading about the car wreck near Los Angeles that tragically claimed the life of the society woman who once upon a time had declared the formal dining configuration in the White House ousted in favor of round tables. I wasn't paying all that much attention to what I was reading, you see, and had coasted three or four paragraphs into the article before realizing I was the protagonist. I was the one some journalist was writing about in the past tense.

My heart clumped like a frightened squirrel locked inside a car trunk. I sat there staring at the newsprint, trying to collect my thoughts, but all I could do was fumble through my pocketbook for some cash, toss it on the table, and hurry back to the newsstand where I bought a copy of every paper the man without a left hand sold. The second I entered my apartment I dropped them in a bunch on the living room floor and squatted over them, gathering courage, then plunged in. The more I read, the more my worst suspicions were confirmed. Some had had happier childhoods than I, some sadder. One of me had taken up flying a month ago but disappeared in a Cessna somewhere near Nantucket. One had received the first bullet intended for Jack and was allegedly lying in a coma somewhere in a private clinic in Caracas. A third had become a heroin addict in Washington, D. C., a fourth a news anchorwoman in the northwest, a fifth had hanged herself in Pittsburgh, a sixth had become the fiancée of a Greek shipping magnate whose unlikely first name was Aristotle. It went on and on. There must have been a dozen of me, maybe more, each drifting through a different life.

Squatting in my living room, surrounded by papers, I recalled coming awake in my nightgown in the middle of the night in my room at the White House, and how I had just stood there watching myself cleaving, coming apart like amoebae do under the microscope. I thought about each one wafting past me toward the door and out into the world and I found myself beginning to remember what they remembered, recollecting moments from lives that I—this I, I mean—had never actually experienced, but, in some alternate cluster of natural laws, might have. I saw Jack had been a faithful husband in many versions of our marriage. In some, he wasn't simply feigning when he threw that football through the autumn afternoon with the kids out on the lawn of our house on the Massachusetts coast, wasn't just constructing himself for the cameras. He was really loving it, loving every moment we were together as a family. And sometimes it wasn't Jack at all, but another man, and sometimes that man was kind and sometimes the opposite. And sometimes there was no man at all. Some of me were growing old alone. Some had never married. And some had married and divorced and remarried and cheated and become successful businesswomen, actors, doctors, fashion designers, models. Many met many famous people in the United States and Europe. One never finished high school. And one had three children and died from Hodgkins disease on May 19, 1994, dreaming perhaps of the way that faithless Jack bent toward her like a Hollywood star that first time to kiss her on the lips.

That very night I packed up my suitcases, rode the elevator down to the lobby, walked out the front door of the building with the lovely view of Central Park, and hailed a cab to the airport. I didn't look back. And here I am, almost forty years later, sitting on the veranda of a small hotel with thatched-roof cottages surrounding its main lodge overlooking a sunny beach and blazing blue ocean somewhere in the British West Indies. I'm sipping an icy piña colada and am already thinking about ordering another. I'm single. I'm happy. My money is gradually running out, but I'm not worried. Something will happen. Something always does. I weigh 246 pounds. My new name is something you wouldn't recognize. I don't think much about the old days. I can't remember them very well even when I put my mind to it. Instead, I try to concentrate on the small acts that might constitute an imagined afternoon—what will I drink next, eat, will I decide to take a short stroll or swim on this beach or another. That's enough. Because I know, leaning back, eyes closed against the shocking light, that there are plenty of me in the world, more than enough, and they can easily get along without this one, and that at least some of them are this very second leading something very close to perfect lives.

Interrupted Reading

1.) *BECAUSE THE BEGINNING of the beginning is an unloaded camera, a shiny new sports car in your driveway, a small-handed wave that may or may not be the wave from a little blond girl who may or may not be your sister three hundred yards off the coast in the boiling surf and gaining distance:*

He hears someone at the
No.
I think I hear someone at the
That's not it.
You think you hear someone at your

                              You answer your front door
and
    And what?
You answer your front door and a little boy dressed like a little man dressed like a bright red, white, and blue superhero, no, a svelte, ravishing medieval princess, no, a thumb-nosed hunchback from last season's television hit, yes, that's it, extends his pillowcase at you and demands candy in a not-wholly-congenial polyp-throated voice.

2.) *Because the beginning after the beginning of the beginning becomes time on fire, the thematics of an escalator:*

The light
When are we?

The light has already grayed out by 4:30.

And where?

A poison tinge from the Turnpike peps the air around you.

Do you have more?

Up and down the block scale-model pro-wrestlers, mutants, valentine-headed space aliens,

Lovely turn of phrase: valentine-headed.

and a lone Apache warrior hustle between split levels, plastic scarecrows, inverted-ice-cream-cone hay bundles and pumpkin arrangements. Fleets of alert mothers cruise in resplendent off-road utility vehicles that will never leave pavement. Pathfinders. Grand Cherokees. Having retrieved their children, they will drive directly to the local mall where artificially cheerful policemen will x-ray the hauls for signatures of malice.

3.) *Because the beginning after the beginning after the beginning (though nowhere near the middle) provides yesterday, the waving girl's name (Sarah ... no, Shauna, Shiloh ... let's call her Sarah), the density of the past tense and thereby complication of the present:*

Tonight marks your last in what legally ceases to be your house in fewer than fourteen hours. Everything around you except a lamp, some rumpled bedding, and a sleeping bag in the living room is boxed or draped with sheets. Even the sound has changed, giving you the impression of standing alone in an empty airplane hangar.

The little boy in front of you impatiently clears his polypoid throat. Snaggy Scree chocolate-and-bubble-gum bar in hand, you look down at him and think about complimenting his costume. It's one of the best you've seen since the spectacles commenced this afternoon just past 3:00. The clothes themselves aren't much: plaid wool sports coat, buttoned white shirt, loose gray wool pants tied with a length of rope, blazingly white techno sneakers. But the mound that rises over his left shoulder, almost ripping through that sports coat, is impressive, as is the way he has built up the skin over his sunken right eye into a cartilaginous lump. The cleft lip and brown-fringed teeth are nothing short of remarkable.

Your glance drifts over his shaved squarish head. Across the street a mother flashes her Ford Explorer's headlights in a intricate code to attract the attention of a chubby, squat Darth Vader and an oversized mushroom busy comparing stashes on the curb. Waving, Darth Vader waddles forward.

4.) *Because Sarah's hand, let's settle on Sarah, the cusps of dirt beneath her chewed fingernails, the inexplicable small red rash … no, birthmark … no, bruise on her upper arm.*

Tomorrow morning the movers arrive. By noon you'll be somewhere near Scranton on route 80, shooting west, because in a sense you can't think of anything else to do.

You grew up fifteen minutes from here in River Edge, attended high school in Oradell and college in New Brunswick and married in Hackensack and worked for almost sixteen years at a technology park in Teaneck and now you're going to leave this house, the east, your wife, Lola, who has, if the truth be known, already left you, though, if asked, you wouldn't be able to clearly articulate any specific reasons.

How does this make you feel? You imagine, standing there with the Snaggy Scree, Superduper Jaggy Large Size, that your heart is
    What?

that your heart is the black box flight recorder from a 747 and you wonder if it will ever reveal any significant information upon inspection.

Glare from the Ford's headlights washes across the left half of the little boy's face in front of you as the 4x4 swings heavily around in the street, halts, and Darth Vader clambers aboard.

The passenger door fumps shut, which is when you realize the little boy in front of you illuminated in the garish splash isn't

5.) *Because the only successful stories—of which this assuredly isn't one—are about two bodies engaged in the conservation of matter, because the way the mother splashes into the surf, the way her husband follows on her heels, how this is called the beginning of the middle.*

The little boy in front of you, you see in the garish splash, isn't really a little boy at all. He isn't dressed *like* a hunchback. He's wearing a lilac five-o'clock shadow and his hands are calloused hammers and a great kyphos protrudes like a vestigial second head directly behind his left ear.

6.) *Because speech is scene and scene is what Sarah's parents yell as they push to-ward their receding child.*

Get away from here, you tell him. Beat it.

You swing the door shut but the hunchback dwarf kicks out his foot and obstructs its arc. He's impressively strong for his dimensions. The door bounces open. His pillowcase bulges with hodgepodge booty like a potato sack.

Hand over the Snaggy Scree, he says.

In the cozy yellow foyer light, you notice each of his knuckles has a greenish-blue letter tattooed on it. The left-hand spells out M-O-R-E, the right-hand H-A-T-E.

Get off my porch, you say, attempting to sound noteworthy.

Gimme the goddamn candy bar.

You estimate his violence capacity, ask: What are you, kidding? Is that what you are? Look at you. You know what I'm giving you? I'm giving you exactly dick, is what I'm giving you.

One of his eyes doesn't close all the way when he blinks.

I'm asking you nicely, you putz, he says. Gimme the fucking candy bar.

Fuck you.

Fuck *you*. You want I should show you crazy? Because I'll show you crazy. I'll show you fucking *batshit*.

I want you should get off my property, is what I want.

A swarm of television sets with children's legs skitters onto your side-walk, takes one look at the confrontation escalating, pauses, reconsiders, and skitters off into the maturing dusk.

I'm giving you precisely shit, is what I'm giving you, precisely, you say. Where you get off impersonating a fucking tot or whatever the hell you call them?

I'm going nowhere till I get my goddamn candy bar. Which I'm not repeating twice. Cuz you just say the word. Seriously. Look at me. I'm pleading here. You want crazy?

He reviews me.

What? he says, suspicious.

What what? you say.

He squints. Or blinks. It's impossible to tell.

You saying I'm nothing to be scared of? he asks. Is *that* what you're saying?

I'm saying I'll call the police, is what I'm saying, if you don't leave my premises here by the count of three.

Son of a *chickenshit*, he says.

The dwarf drops his pillowcase. Candy clatters across cement. He crouches and lifts his hammer fists.

His thumb-nose grinches.

7.) *Because the first wobble and clunk that announces your blown tire, the first dip below the churning gray water.*

The dwarf reaches into his back pocket and when his hammer fist appears again there's nothing … no, a switchblade, no, a slick midnight-blue snub-nosed revolver stuck in it. It reminds you of the kind detectives used in police dramas from your childhood.

Only you can't tell whether it's an authentic slick midnight-blue snub-nosed revolver or a toy that only looks like a slick midnight-blue snub-nosed revolver.

What did I just say? he says.

You realize in the few minutes you've been talking the dusk has pixelated into evening. Another few pulses, and this instant will have become the past. A smile seeps into your features.

What? he says, astonished. You think this is some kind of fucking joke? You think this is some fuh—

You reach out and slam the heavy door in his face.

8.) *Because sun-sparkle on slate-blue waves off the Pacific coast, the Pacific coast or the Atlantic coast, sometimes such details not being especially important.*

After the fact, you don't remember starting to move your arm.

9.) *The feeling in the pit of your hope that you can no longer control your careening vehicle as it tugs into the lanes of traffic speeding toward you.*

Immediately diminutive clumping commences on the other side. The hunchback dwarf is furious. He's trying to kick down your door, chip through it with his switchblade, no, his real or fake gun butt, trying to ram through with his shoulder and his curses and his elbows.

Next, suddenly as it explodes, time stills.

The revolver, it occurs to you, can't be loaded. If it were loaded, it would have gone off. Unless it isn't a revolver. You swim through several additional thoughts, tabulating, then bend forward and consult the peephole.

Through the fisheye lens you see the dwarf cringed in pain. He's cuddling his left foot in both palms. The gun rests on the cement among a circus of splattered jawbreakers, candy corn, sticks of chewing gum, rolls of Life Savers, peanut butter cups, specialty-jelly-bean boxes, and a single wobbling glazed apple which revolves unsteadily to the very edge of the stoop, hesitates, and plunks off.

You watch the hunchback dwarf bounce less and less. A minute, and he concludes. He lowers his foot gently to the concrete, stands erect as his tangled spine will let him, considers the evening sky. He places his hammer hands on his lower back and cracks it, then kneels like an old man claiming a nickel in the middle of the street and begins sweeping together his loot.

10.) *Because the beginning of the end is the tiredness in a bystander's eyes, the unyielding feeling that you could have always done more for Sarah.*

Watching his homuncular form diminish, you feel instantly bad. You should open the door and invite him in. Look at him. Look at him out there. What would it have taken for you to play dumb, act like a human being?

Except as he prepares to gimp into the street five boys, fifteen or sixteen years old, emerge from behind a massive evergreen bush and surround him. They're dressed only as themselves. They're wearing black wool ski caps and hyperbolically baggy jeans and white t-shirts three times too large even though it's the last day of October.

They say something and push him.

He pushes back.

A struggle flares. One teen yanks the overfed pillowcase from the hunchback dwarf's grip and holds it just out of his reach. He leaps for it, once, then backs up and brings his gun into view. A passing Geo Tracker slows down. Another teen drops to all fours behind him and a third shoves the hunchback dwarf over into a pile of leaves banked on the curb.

He receives four or five eggs in the chest and then the boys have vanished.

11.) *Because in the end the man crashing through the waves is sleeping with his wife's best friend or he isn't, the best friend is either a boy or a girl or he or she isn't, because neither parent will forget this day, the one on which they lost their daughter or didn't, the day the man died trying to reach her or didn't, the day Sarah suffered brain damage or didn't, the day she never knew anything was out of the ordinary or did, she wondering why in the world her parents were running along the beach, what they were shouting about, you can never figure out the mechanics of the old, why the others were gathering with them, because she was just playing, because someone either caught it all on video or didn't, because those few minutes appeared later that day on YouTube or didn't, because however you choose to tell her story the wife will always reach down one warm summer morning in the shower stall and brush across that lump, the one larger and harder than she ever thought such a lump could be, though she had always been careful to perform self-examinations, or maybe had never been, and in any version you tell she will then close her eyes and palpate that lump in simple wonder at the abrupt fact of it, then do no more than comfortably tilt her head back into the cool chlorinated spray, hoping to enjoy this passing instant as fully as possible.*

The hunchback attempting to brush himself off and disappearing into the swarms of other teratoids hustling up and down that suburban block in northern New Jersey.

Which is the last thing you see as you retire from the peephole, turn and stroll through your house that is no longer your house, clicking off lights and touching things that won't be touchable tomorrow.

After a while you lie down among the rumpled bedding.

Minutes later, the doorbell rings.

Minutes later, the doorbell rings again.

The Doll

AFTER WE WERE DONE DOING IT in a manner in which we had
never done it before, she rolled onto her side and asked:

What's next?

I, remaining on my stomach, said: What?

This was a frisky blue Sunday afternoon and we were in her apartment
on the floor beneath the kitchen table. Several chairs were lying on their
sides. The table wasn't where I had remembered it being. A piquant scent
of cucumber and I want to say olive oil confused the atmosphere.

Her apartment or my apartment. I don't remember which, actually.
Her apartment, my apartment, or, for that matter, a friend's who was away
for the weekend and had lent us his. A man named Robert, say.

All the same, there was clearly a sense of upended apartmentness surrounding us.

The point not being where we were, but rather the gist of her question,
which took me by surprise because I was at that very moment busy per-
spiring diligently and thinking less diligently about what we had just done,
and we were taking turns employing Kleenexes from a pale blue box of
them with a floral design which sat on the tiled floor beside us but which
not long ago had sat, I seem to recall without any real conviction, on the
bathroom sink or on the desk in the foyer, where our afternoon's undertaking had originated, I want to say, and I was concomitantly busy wiping
off various leaky fluids and/or beginning to collect vegetable refuse that
had aggregated in our vicinity.

I saw all this, for some reason, from a third-person point of view, as if I were standing in the kitchen door, the scene stripped of its normal saturation and hues.

It surprised me, her question, because we had been doing it now for I want to say three months, though undeniably it had been no more than five, six would be a maximum, and we had done it each time, or very nearly, in interesting places with from my perspective interesting apparatuses while utilizing unfamiliar postures, each one of which—posture or apparatus—possessing a metaphoric name with great connotative resonance.

Airplanes. Rooftops. A stall in the women's restroom at the Holocaust Museum in a city other than the one you're thinking of when I say the Holocaust Museum.

Double Helixes, Quantum Foam, Rabbit Mouths.

I'm not particularly proud of that, by the way. The Holocaust Museum, I mean. I'm not particularly unproud of that, either.

It surprised me, as I say, her question, because we had been doing it now for I want to say three months, though undoubtedly it had been for no more than five or seven—since, that is, we met at an independent film in an independent-film-showing theater downtown, whose title, plot, and general theme escape me. We were the only ones there. That part doesn't escape me. It doesn't escape me, either, how everything smelled of mildew and artificially flavored buttered popcorn.

We were the only ones there, or very nearly so, perhaps there were one or two others scrunched down in the back, and yet we serendipitously took conterminous seats because we were both committed to achieving the most efficacious viewing range from the not-all-that-large-independent-film-showing-theater screen.

A Japanese film, it now comes to me, subtitled in English, but you didn't need the subtitles to understand any of it because almost no one spoke, although many groaned or screamed, and there was no plot except for the fact that there was this man, an average Joe, who turns into a machine one day for no apparent reason, and then this woman, who is quite probably the man's lover, although this is by no means indisputable, who also turns into a machine one day for no apparent reason, unless the man was imagining the woman turning into a machine, and maybe even imagining himself turning into a machine, which always remained in my mind an acceptable possibility, or maybe there was even a third-party consciousness dreaming the immachinating couple, who knows, really, or it's not totally out of the realm of probability that I'm simply summoning the wrong movie.

The point being merely this: that I recall, I believe, much jump-cutting, and, during one scene, the man, or the imagined man, doing it with the woman, or the imagined woman, with a three-foot-long steel penis that revolved like a drill and was shaped like a dunce's cap, if you can imagine such a thing, and, during another scene, both the woman or the imagined woman and the man or the imagined man ending up turning into parts of the same machine—a tank, I want to say, or, in any event, a tank-like mobile object—and the man speaking one of the perhaps ten lines in the film.

I've never been so happy, he said.

In Japanese, of course.

And that's how we met: she starting, first, by sort of humming at the strangeness of the movie under her breath. Soon she began fully vocalizing about the strangeness, sometimes asking questions, perhaps to herself, perhaps to me, it was difficult to tell, and sometimes she developed a running almost sub-vocal analysis centering on the film's sense of power relations and, I want to say, the hermeneutics of desire.

She had purchased, I couldn't help noticing, one of those very large tubs of artificially flavored buttered popcorn that packed the theater with its being-thereness. A vat, actually, into which you could place a small dog. A Chihuahua, for example.

About half an hour into the film I began to answer her questions, never taking my eyes off the not-large screen.

I was aware of her stealing glances at me, initially, like maybe I wasn't talking to her but to myself, just like she was talking to maybe herself and not to me, only then she plainly decided I wasn't dangerous, or I wasn't particularly dangerous, and she began to take exception with my reading, which centered mostly on the film's critique of our culture's fetish of technology, and, two hours later, we began doing it in my apartment.

Once upon a time, I should add, I was a philosophy major. My apartment or her apartment. Which was, I want to say, between three and eight months ago, and without a doubt no more than let us call it nine.

What's next? she asked, having rolled onto her side and this—the question, not the rolling—as I have already mentioned, surprised me.

Because, if the truth be known, I was running low on ideas, and this question suggested to me as I wiped off various leaking fluids that she might be running out of ideas, too, because she had never asked it before, this question, I mean.

Over the course of the last nine or ten months, eleven was a maximum, I had dressed up in a miscellany of interesting apparel and discovered, among other things, how fetching I looked in a pair of red pumps and black corset, and so had she, and we had posted images of ourselves engaged in the manipulation of those interesting apparatuses while utilizing myriad unfamiliar and thereby exciting postures on the internet on diverse interesting amateur-submitted-images sites, and there was obviously that time we did it in an elevator halted between floors of a skyscraper, she dressed as a ponytailed school girl in All-Star hightops and I as a Nazi officer—what American didn't at some point enact *that* cliché?—and once we invited her friend or my friend whose apartment we were perhaps at that moment using, let us call him Robert, and his wife, his wife or girlfriend, let us call her Robert, too, to join us in a seedy hotel room in a seedy section of the city with a box of matches and an alleged snuff film featuring a bound and gagged Asian teen, that old warhorse, and as most couples do at some point in their relationship we put an ad in the paper for those what do you call them little people and would have video-taped our assignation had anyone replied to said ad, which they didn't.

In other words I think you could say we were in love. Yes, I'm sure I think you could call it that. From the day we met we pretty much never left each other's side.

Except, of course, to go to work. Me in a Kinko's uptown, she in a Wendy's downtown. Work, eat, once in a long while socialize with friends or colleagues on a one-to-one basis, travel infrequently into the countryside, evacuate our respective bowels diurnally, wander the streets at night yelling at the moon, read, listen to music, bike, skate, and, upon the rarest of occasions, do it with someone else.

One could say we were inseparable, except for that.

And hence when she rolled onto her side, propped her head in her palm, and asked *What's next?* it is I suspect no surprise how surprised I was.

Her eyes were hazel, by the way. This seems an opportune moment to mention such an important detail. The sort of non-metaphoric hazel which is, if you study it carefully, as I did, multiple times, browner toward the edges of the contractile membrane and then increasingly brownish-yellow and then yellowish-brown as you move toward the fat period of the black pupil.

Her eyes were hazel and her hair shaved right down to gray skin with a razor every morning.

Unless she was wearing one of her wigs, in which case her hair was sometimes shoulder length and sometimes done in pigtails or ponytails or in Egyptian fashion and sometimes in a prim beehive from the early Sixties like my fifth-grade teacher, Mrs. Robert, and always in an interesting color one tends to associate with selections of fingernail polish rather than, say, hair.

Her eyes were hazel and her breasts were boyish and she was thinner than what might be considered in some medical circles wholly healthy and we were, with those very few exceptions already mentioned, inseparable, and so I saw myself that frisky Sunday afternoon, as if my point-of-view were situated in the doorway of the kitchen, and not beneath the table among overturned chairs, cease wiping and say: What?

What's next? she repeated.

Oh, I said. Oh.

I rolled from my stomach onto my back and then hoisted myself into a hunched, cross-legged sitting position.

You could see her lover trying to think. It wasn't a pretty sight. Finally, however, he cleared his throat and replied, a little evasively: You'll see.

I'll see?

You'll see.

When?

Soon.

How soon?

Tomorrow soon.

I work tomorrow.

Tomorrow night, then. Meet me at my place after work tomorrow night.

The boy-breasted woman continued looking at the scrawny red-haired man for another few seconds with her hazel eyes that seemed to lack very much I suppose you could call it emotion, then she half-smiled and rolled away from him and stood and collected her clothes, most of which turned out, startlingly, to be scattered throughout the living room, dressed, and left without saying goodbye.

I watched that guy as he finished cleaning up and then I watched him return to his apartment across town, unless this was his apartment, obviously, in which case he stayed where he was, being at home already.

The following evening, I watched me pick up some things at the corner market after work, hurry back to someone's apartment, almost surely mine, throw together a green salad with a light vinaigrette dressing, and sauté some onions and mushrooms in butter in a wok, some butter or some olive oil, this part always presents a number of mnemonic challenges for me—at which point the doorbell rang, or there was a knock at the door, and in any event I watched the scrawny red-haired man trot down the hall in his terrycloth bathrobe and answer the ring or knock, whichever it might have been, then accompany the boy-breasted woman in her short black dress, black high-topped combat boots, and shiny purple Betty Boop wig back into the kitchen, where they worked in harmonious tandem to set an elegant table, light two romantic white vanilla-scented candles, and the scrawny red-haired man poured the boy-breasted woman and himself a glass of Life-Saver-red wine, led her over to the counter, and raised his glass in a toast.

Then he showed her the wooden cutting board on the counter by which they stood, a short time after which they ate each other's little toes (sans toenails) with a tincture of paprika mixed with the onion, mushrooms, and olive oil to enliven the comestibles.

The amputation was realized with a meat cleaver designed and manufactured in Europe—Germany, I want to say—and was followed by a sharp if not wholly unexpected discomfort, which was itself followed by an almost indescribable euphoria and intense focusing of one's perceptive abilities that obtained long after the bandages and cotton gauze had been applied to stanch the flow of what have you.

Bones comprising the little toe bring soft-shell crabs to mind.

It was always difficult to pick a favorite philosopher.

Afterward I followed us up the street of let us call them brownstones to the bus stop, we were hobbling slightly, and watched as we kissed each other beneath a halogen lamp crawling with large commas and broken brackets.

Next day the scrawny red-haired man hobbled through Kinko's in an animated daydream. His eyes had the acute look to them of someone playing the last minute of a video game when he or she is maybe three clicks away from attaining the final level and let us say saving the princess. He misplaced orders, employed the wrong plastic binding on two separate instances.

Shooting incident, he answered when his colleagues asked.

His boss's name, I should take this opportunity to mention, was Robert.

The scrawny red-haired man almost never talked to any them except to refer to immediate matters of business. He had always kept to himself. It was therefore with little effort that he continued keeping to himself now.

Shooting incident, he answered, and then, two weeks later: hatchet incident.

Shaving incident, hedge-trimming incident, jack-o'-lantern-carving incident.

In the beginning it all seemed more natural than one might perhaps suppose. Then it didn't. Then he stopped caring. Then they began avoiding him. Robert, Robert, Robert, Robert, Robert, and Robert began making large arcs around him when they felt the insuperable need to pass. Then he stopped going to work.

In larger cases boiling water achieved both effective cauterization and a certain compounding of one's overall sense of euphoria, which the boy-breasted woman in sundry wigs began to refer to affectionately as The Angel's Kiss.

Wittgenstein, of course. Sartre.

Not that anyone reads the latter anymore.

Sadly.

The Angel's Kiss is upon me, she would sometimes announce, trembling or shaking, folded into a fetal position on the floor, eyes rolled back in her head.

And so events in our love story moved inexorably toward the commonplace happy conclusion, except that some things didn't. One's big toes, we discovered, for instance, provide a greater sense of balance than the layman often suspects, and, once one's feet are gone, up to the knees, the idea of gainful employment pretty much flies out the window, as does the notion, I want to add, of popping down to the corner market to pick up this or that.

I should also remark that one should never attempt to remove one's genitals, one's genitals or one's mammary glands, when one is fully conscious.

Yet what is truly remarkable is how little effort it takes one to meet one's basic dietary needs, particularly if one rounds out one's meals with a daily vitamin supplement. Pay your rent and utilities in advance: this is a no-brainer, really. Stockpile supplies. Remember to save one's tongue until one feels one no longer has anything of specific interest to articulate.

Once upon a time I was a philosophy major and once upon a time she was a film studies major, both at the University other than the one you're thinking of when I say the University.

It's a small world.

One partner should obviously also save an arm, hand, and at least two fingers, one of which should be that often-cited opposable thumb, if either partner is set on, let us say, keeping a journal of ones thoughts and feelings or composing poems or lyrics about this introspective time in one's life, and appendages will furthermore prove pivotal in the execution of The Scalping.

Which is where they are now, where we are now, she and I, two torsos and two heads gurgling happily on someone's futon. It is dark in here. It may be a weekend. There is inarguably some breathing taking place.

In any case the saddest thing about the present, it occurs to that scrawny red-haired man as he not very neatly jots his last impressions on this yellow legal pad on my stomach, these last impressions, mine, is how, when making love there is always a limit case to the quantity of occasions one can in fact do it and a conceptual boundary to the operations that comprise such an activity, this being the one secret all directors of pornographic videos never want you to understand. Beyond that is The Angel's Kiss, and, beyond that, every single time, nothing at all.

Where Does the Kissing End?

TELL ME A STORY I SAYS laying there in the almost black and my
mama she says *go to bed, girl,* and i says *tell me a story first, mama* and my
mama she says *go to bed now, you hear* and i says *just one* and my mama she
says rolling her eyes toward heaven up in the almost black with that way
she has of sucking her cigarette and letting its smoke spike out her nose
like a cow on a cold autumn morning *just one, girl, just one and then to sleep*
and so commences to spin me the most beautiful i ever done heard about
this kind and handsome prince who done got turned into a toad by a evil
witch with hairy warts on her face and pink knuckles like tree skin cuz he
did not mind her and this blindingly pretty princess who only wore white
lace and done righted him into what he truly was with a gentle and pure
kiss which sent the angels above to weeping and that was it that was all
cuz i could not sleep that night no matter what but stayed awake after my
mama she done finished telling and stayed awake after she done stood and
touched my forehead with her rough dry palm thinking i was gone away
and stayed awake through the carbon hours the opal hours the lilac ones
aware-dreaming of that sweetest kiss bar none which brought the world
up short and changed everything god calls human everything he does not
and made the landscape re-picture itself so many times the landscape began
hurting cuz that is what real love can do cuz that is what the touch of a
princess can do it can make you see how a prince can return from the red
undertow we call living and so i did not wake up cuz i never went to sleep
for happiness but when i heard my mama grinding coffee in the kitchen
and slamming the fridge and feeding our kitties partly cloudy rainy and

thunder i slipped out from under my sheets ran down the hall in my panties slid onto my stool at the table and ate silent like as i hardly knew how no more cuz i was still aware-dreaming of that perfectness even as my mama she asks me how i slept cuz i had nothing more to say cuz that was the rightest story i suppose i will ever hear in my entire life bar none and so done finished i slid off my stool and slipped on my pretty flower dress with the white collar and flipflops and smack went the trailer door behind me saying *playing* when my mama she done asked after me where i was going to *down by the swamp* as she done told me to mind my feet her voice dropping off behind me like a memory you can't quite remember which is where i done aimed directly the sky all blue like precious stones in the prince's cape and the sun humming like a swarm of yellow jackets behind my eyes and the air hot-damp and riotous with fragrances thinking about my mama calls it *elation* thinking about *elation* and lace gowns that you never ever take off following the shrimp-pink dirt path behind our trailer into the woods where the earth feels spongy and cicadas put their bodies into your brain like the static between radio stations and you leave one way of seeing for another cuz everything there seems so much more *real* cuz it is all so what is the word *overstated* which is what you are both thinking and not thinking when you spot the frog on the fallen tree trunk in the shallow avocado-scummed water so you make a large arc and angle in from behind where the ground is still semi-firm and you crouch and duck-waddle then sit in absolute stillness for the count of ten twenty thirty and then see your hands swooping in from the sides so fast they are not your hands anymore but alarmed swallows and you never thought about setting them in motion but even as that idea flickers up at you the frog is in your cupped palms that were birds and at your lips which you worry might be too dry like mama's cuz of the sunshine but it is what is inside that counts and makes the red undertow roll away from the shore of your soul as you kiss quick a brush-kiss like as with the boys brush-kissing on the play-ground during recess in the great telephone-line of kooties and nothing whatsoever happens but this does not surprise you cuz you know such a minor gesture will never be sufficient for a prince even though mice are rushing among your organs cuz it is not fully felt somehow not in the curve behind your knees between your toes in the tail you cannot see yet know forms the base of your spine because they told you in school so you bring the frog back to your mouth again and this time you can feel its muscular nervousness in your cupped palms feel the animal's feet scuffling in the cage which is you and you open your mouth and open a black hole between your thumbs and carefully lovingly insert your tongue into it lick what you find there and your breath goes away and the yellow-jacket-sun unfolds behind your eyes and the moist granular skin not unlike your mama's hands after vanilla lotion the lungs pulsing like as fly wings the taste honey-salt and green and a kind of frightened agitation within your palms fidgeting back-kicking going nowhere though you go everywhere and give it another long gentle lick-kiss which has nothing whatsoever to do with those that you have till this day delivered upon others nor those that have been delivered upon you and you can sense the red undertow withdrawing feel how this is righter than anything you have ever thought till that is you retract your tongue and wait and stoop and fan your fingers open and set the frog among weeds and watch him watch with his dead gold eyes watching and wait till you realize only gradually that the world has not changed not one mite because the frog is still the frog and you are still yourself and the sky is still blue and your heart is still your heart till you realize only gradually that you have guessed wrong and so you rise into the rays your teacher says are all around you and inside you too and shut your eyes and listen to the bumblebees the cicadas the intermittent chitters scattershot through the branches braiding above you which puts you in mind of your mama how she sometimes collapses into herself like an imploding building on the news how sometimes after dinner you find her all alone outside in the lawn chair smoking head tilted back eyes closed as if she can watch the twilight through her lids and you ask her what she is doing and she tells you still not opening her eyes *nothing, girl* only that word does not mean what it means it means something so big and black it can hardly fit into a sentence and her lack of saying says more than her saying ever could the sun bit by bit turning itself off and the evening bit by bit turning itself on and the oversweet summer breeze stirring for maybe fifteen minutes without cooling and you go back into the trailer to watch television or listen to the radio trying not to think about all this thinking but after a while you go out again to see and she is still there still sitting in the lawn chair precisely as you left her smoking with her head tilted back eyes closed and so you push on into the woods thistles skunk cabbage elephant grass where the path forks and re-forks like a car with its windshield smashed while the sun goes on getting louder the atmosphere tropical like as the inside of a dog's mouth and the you that is me walks singing all the songs i can think of and some that i have to make up till i come upon the pond which is without shore or bank but simply eases into being right under my feet one minute not there and there the next the grass wetter and wetter and then drops off into hot chocolate as far as the eye can see and so i crab around the side that is not a side quiet as a garter snake cuz my mama she says i do not have a daddy and i says that is the silliest thing i ever done heard cuz everybody got a daddy somewheres and she says *YOU* don't, *girl* and i says but everybody got a daddy somewheres and she says *you just forget about such bullshit right now, you hear* and she even said that word like she was not thinking of saying it nor not saying it and so the you that is me walks sing-crabbing along the side till i spot another frog and get down on my hands and knees and crawl through tall limp grass and become a statue and count ten twenty thirty and pounce and there it is in my hands the prince and i repeat what i done before only more carefully lovingly yet except this frog is larger than the first and stronger and at the last second i decide to put my mouth over the hole between my thumbs and just for a single human pulse its amphibious head slips between my lips and everything turns pure white behind my eyes it is out again and frozen and nothing but a frog and i confess though i do it in tiny additions sidling up on the notion that this process will take longer than i suspected so i set this frog which is only a frog down and move on till i find another and repeat the process and move on till i find another and repeat before long discovering i can begin to tell the difference between tastes textures smells this frog's back skin or ear plate more marshy than the last or less lumpy or more oily and this strikes me with the force of revelation cuz till then every frog has been the same frog every frog only one frog but now each is only itself the light passing above me and so i move along the shore that was not a shore scooping up frogs that are not frogs and kissing each and every one as if it is the most weighty thing i can do except when i pick up one the size of my fist and infold its head in my mouth and put it down again i think i see out the edge of my seeing a rustling in the limp grass and next thing a water rat sliding through the brackishness where the frog had been and i commence wondering if maybe inside some frogs are neither princes nor frogs but other creatures for instance ghosts of say deer or fish or dead kitties like partly cloudy rainy and thunder or maybe the souls of people who have accidentally fallen into the swamp and drowned cuz they did not mind their feet like their mamas had done told them and maybe even my daddy somewheres out there i remember the sandskin of his beard think i remember cuz he had gotten so sad waiting for me and my mama to return to him waiting for me and my mama to phone or knock on his screen door that *his* soul finally just gave up and walked away from its body and that is what i found myself thinking when squatting by the pond that was not a pond cuz i looked up and saw the day above the trees was all of a sudden failing and i had not noticed the hours going by not listened to my appetite growing inside me not understood the regret of the light bleaching away sky becoming lemon rind becoming the tender flesh beneath your eyes and bird chitter and i could hear the oceanic rise of croaking and came to understand if only for a instant how many frogs existed in this swamp around me and how many swamps existed in this county around me and how many counties existed in this state around me and how many states existed in this country around me and how many countries existed in this world around me and how many worlds existed in this galaxy around me and how many galaxies existed in this universe around me and in that second i did not turn back toward my mama's trailer but continued my sing-crabbing along the side of the pond that was not a pond wondering somewhere so far back in my mind that it almost seemed like someone else's *where does the kissing end?*

New Fictions

(2004-2013)

Art Lecture

1. OR, FOR ARGUMENT'S SAKE, the other thing.
   a. Rust art being vapored with the taste of trains.
   b. Paris, for instance.
      i. The wind was bitter.
         1. Vienna.
         2. London.
         3. Patterson, New Jersey.
   c. Before which many Christian martyrs were demoted to the status of smoke.

2. Needless to say there has always been the question of hands.

3. Outside our local indie-movie house, a bearded man in an army jacket plays his cello at twilight.
   a. Poorly.
   b. People provide him with supernumerary change.
   c. After which art turns into glass.
      i.   A sparkling blue-white depthlessness.
      ii. Coffee. Oranges. Chocolate.

4. Once there was a lot of sweat, music, offal, and prayer, and then that stopped.

    a. Eos mistakenly asked Zeus for eternal life for Tithonus without remembering to ask for eternal life's compelling corollary: eternal youth.

    b. X-ray art smelling like sunshine in your hair after shampooing with Prell, only from the inside out.

    c. Kafka strolls across Prague's town square, head down, nibbling a hangnail, imagining two fried-egg eyes pancaked in a black pan.

    d. The shock of discovering the meaning of the word scaphism.

       i. The joy of the boisterous human imagination.

       ii. Be studious in your profession, and you will be learned.

          1. Ben.

          2. Franklin.

5. The rabbit as a rule will scream only once in its life, usually at the end.

6. We should always be new in the neighborhood.

    a. Berlin. New York.

    b. There being no way to save memory.

       i. There is no way to remain where you are.

          1. St. Petersburg.

          2. Zurich.

          3. (Let red be your destroyer.)

    c. God is standing in my wardrobe, sorting ties, some say, a moment before the rabbit screams.

    d. Marcel Duchamp gives up painting in favor of chess nearly fifty years before he returns to his own planet.

7. Hands, shoulders, shiny buttons. Her panties. The black bull with the body of a man, twirling in the breeze like wind chimes, tinkling.

8. There are always openings, you see.

9. Repetition can be dangerous.

    a. Repetition can be dangerous.

    b. Or not.

10. Henri Bergson: we cannot experience the present because it is always-already something else by the time we have processed it.
    a. To live is to experience the relentlessly ongoing expression of the past tense.
        i. The elevator: 1793.
        ii. Cinnamon: 2000 B.C.
        iii. The original Macintosh: 1984.
            1. You will never need more than 128k of memory.
                a. Bill.
                b. Gates.
    b. The Age of Being Afraid.
        i. *Viz.*: ours.
    c. Before which many Japanese people were demoted to the status of energy emitted in the form of subatomic particles.
    d. Et cetera.

11. On September 22, 1823, the Angel Moroni visited Joseph Smith for the first time.
    a. And told him about golden plates buried in a stone box in a hillside.
        i. A few miles from his home.
            1. In western New York.
            2. Palmyra.
        ii. Theophany: the appearance of a deity to a human.
            1. Duct tape.
            2. The clanking invention of hope.
    b. Moroni had buried the plates before he died after a great battle between two pre-Columbian civilizations.
        i. Moroni was a man.
        ii. Then he was an angel.
        iii. Then there was Mormonism.
            1. No art originated from this event.
            2. None.
            3. One can live only by forgetting.
    c. Joseph Smith, reports confirm, was unsurprised.

12. Everyone on occasion overhears music seeping in from ambient iPods.
    a. The passenger jet a bright white snowflake in a brutal blue sky.
    b. Tokyo. Istanbul. Paris.
    c. The ham, some say.
    d. In May 1961, Piero Manzoni created ninety small cans, placed a small amount of his own feces in each (or perhaps claimed to have done so), sealed the cans, and priced them at the current value of gold: $1.12 per gram.
        i. The most recent one to be auctioned, #19, was sold on 26 February 2007 in the U.S.A.
        ii. For $80,000.
    e. Gingerbread. Licorice.
    f. Pumpkin bread.

13. Czeslaw Milosz: the purpose of poetry being to remind us how difficult it is to remain just one person. A feel-good thought.
    a. Cloud art: white with a whiff of French vanilla.
    b. Clutter art: multihued with the voices of others.
    c. Black edifice art: that which you walk through with your eyes closed.
    d. (What does skin have to do with autobiography?)
    e. Dryads, hot-air balloons, mustard gas, and then that stopped. Et cetera.
    f. The first working television system with electronic scanning of both pickup and display devices: 1928.
        i. Philo Farnsworth.
        ii. Beaver, Idaho.
        iii. Mormon.
        iv. Look it up.

14. Although it could just as well have been Venice.
    a. I.e., the Gatling gun: 1862.
    b. In heaven, all the interesting people are missing.
        i. Friedrich.
        ii. Nietzsche.

c. Life being what it is, one dreams of revenge.
   i.   Paul.
   ii. Gauguin.
d. I can't understand why people are frightened of new ideas; I'm frightened of the old ones.
   i.   John.
   ii. Cage.
e. The sound invisible art makes: a circus of the mind in motion.
   i.   The wind was
   ii. Every unreal artist owns a ruler.
   iii. After which they
f. Monday, some say.

15. The narrative of the writer/serial killer who tears out the still-beating hearts of his victims and inserts the organs into his own chest so that he might learn to experience what others feel.
a. Identity tourism.
b. The dream in which you tell yourself to wake up because this clearly doesn't seem like one of your dreams.

16. Through advanced imaging, below the first painting a second is often revealed.
a. Below the second, a third.
b. Below the third, a fourth.
   i. Below the fourth, et cetera.
      1. Et cetera.
      a. Et cetera.
      b. Et cetera.
         i. Blessed is he who expects nothing.
         ii. For he shall never be disappointed.
            1. Alexander.
            2. Pope.
            3. Q.E.D.

17. Once the films have begun inside our local indie-movie house, the bearded man in the army jacket packs up his cello and scarecrows down the street.

a. In search, say, of a pizza slice.

   i.   Preferably pepperoni.

   ii. With plenty of oregano.

   iii. And napkins.

   iv. Six.

   v. Four.

   vi. One.

      1. Shredded.

      2. Honeydew green.

         a. Tinkling like chimes.

         b. Angel man.

18. But you have to look for them.

a. Otherwise blueberry yogurt.

b. White re-considerations.

c. On Facebook.

19. Once there was existentialism, and then that stopped.

20. On Facebook you receive an invitation to join a group called Nothing.

a. Sarah is soon to be released in a theater near you.

   i.   Coca-cola.

   ii. Milk Duds.

   iii. Good & Plenty.

      1. À-la-mode art feels like mint.

      2. Wish art sounds like

b. Andrew is amazed at several small fluffy coughs flapping around in the hedge outside his window.

c. Paul plots the theft of his own identity.

   i.   The diving bell: 300 B.C.

   ii. The flute: 35,000 B.C.

   iii. In Germany.

    d. Fred refuses to be flummoxed.

      i. Squirming at the memory of the conversation he just had.

        1. Assuming he remembers it correctly.

        2. Assuming the conversation took place to begin with.

        3. Assuming he is Fred.

          a. Jacques Derrida's last words: I love you and am smiling   at you from wherever I am.

          b. The fishing reel: 300 A.D.

21. Or, presumably, the way yellow forgets.

    a. Kafka locating a seat at an outdoor café and quietly ordering an espresso.

    b. Cortés stepping onto the shore of the Yucatan Peninsula and exhaling.

    c. Queen Elizabeth riding through the gates of the palace and briefly sensing what the color orange feels like.

    d. I don't know if God exists, but it would be better for His reputation if He didn't.

      i. Jules.

      ii. Renard.

        1. Edward Kienholz's corpulent, embalmed body is wedged into the front seat of a brown 1940 Packard coupe.

          a. A dollar and deck of cards in his pocket.

          b. A bottle of 1931 Chianti beside him.

          c. The ashes of his dog, Smash, in the trunk.

        2. To the bleat of bagpipes, the Packard, steered by his widow, rolls like a funeral barge into the big hole.

    e. Travelers don't know where they're going; tourists don't know where they've been.

      i. Paul.

      ii. One would have to say.

      iii. Theroux.

      iv. Threadbare lucubrations.

22. And then the honeymoon is over.

a. We stand on the far bank.
   i. Chewing tinfoil.
   ii. Shocked by the visual polyphony of owl pellets.
   iii. The major seventh of desire.
   iv. Onyx storage drums at the Hanford nuclear site.
      1. 200 square miles of contaminated ground water.
      2. Honeybee diaphaneity.
      3. How anguish art deploys heliotrope vowels.
   v. Brightly colored condoms.
   vi. With clown faces printed on them.
b. The gasp as a punctuation mark.

23. When Tithonus could no longer move, no longer lift his limbs, Eos laid him in a chamber behind shining gold doors where he could babble endlessly to himself without disturbing others.

Status Updates

… KAMI HAS KITCHEN FAUCETS that turn in new and disturbing directions. Wayde is wondering what the police are up to across the street. Maeko is making caution do 500 jumping jacks. Nico is in New Jersey. Safa is spoiling the birds with warm bathwater. Chloe is white quiet. Roger is preparing for the robust theater of subtexts that is the Michelson Christmas Eve dinner. Heather is happy. Sara will pay Mother Earth to quit with the fucking snow already. Dixon is trying to convince his dog the cats in the neighborhood aren't out to get her, even though he feels he may be wrong about this. Freya is back from France. Sanjay is running out of time. Calista has 391 different attitudes and logarithmic fragrances, allegedly. Ripley is revising. Shaun is should-ing all over himself. Jack is killing time the old-fashioned way—with a pistol. Elin is not sure whether she prefers Splenda or Nutrasweet. Vicki is feeling vomitous this morning. Tori is laughing at the name of Amish towns with her coworkers: Intercourse, Dildo, Blue Ball. Anna is going running despite what the weather has in mind. David is packing. Daniel soothes crying babies until he walks out of the room and they start crying again. Abbie believes there should be a word (Anglo-Saxon in rootage, naturally) meaning nostalgic for the land of colors. Ramiro got a rock in his eye this morning. Van is still burping up Thai food. Lucian does not want anyone to take seriously the joke he is playing on his Zionist friend. Melissa is off to perform miracles in the kitchen. Percy is telling you something personal here. Dixon's Chihuahua is resisting his peanut-butter-flavored toothpaste. Jacques decides if he can't make his nurses laugh he will make them cry. Trish needs a title. Heather is happy. Wanda feels like every day she's pressured a little bit more into obtaining a Gmail account. Jacob just got older.

Ruby realizes with shame how long it's been since she's washed her hair. Staci is in Santa Cruz. Pamela is in her pajamas. Cathy wants the coughing to stop. Bree believes it's always a mistake reading your ex's blog. Bill believes snarkishness is the new warm-and-fuzzies. Mia would like to have lunch with Marcus Aurelius. Luke is basking in the effulgence of his own laziness. Layla believes there's something a little weird about reading scriptures while sitting in the bathtub. Wanda wonders what part of no-plastic-toys-from-China-please the grandparents don't understand. Ella remains baffled by the 80's. Donald is rocking Doctor Octoroc's 8-Bit Buddha. Lilly loves price adjustments. Doug had a dream last night that involved him climbing a tree in stilettos; he will take this as a sign that he should recycle more. Wayde wonders what the fuck just happened. Knute cannot bend his left knee. Kami is remembering wistfully how much fun it was to shoot pumpkins in the desert on her birthday. Aimee is, to the best of her knowledge. Wesley worries Facebook is like 100,000 too-cute phone calls from people you hardly know. Ryan is fairly sure hell just froze over. Rusti would like to clarify she still wants attention & she still doesn't care whether it's good attention or bad. Penny is feeling prepositional. Sara is afraid she just ate not one, not two, but THREE donuts. Ava admits her addiction to Instagram accounts of well-dressed dogs living in Tokyo is beginning to make her life unmanageable. Freya is frightened there are stains out there that her arsenal of cleansers cannot tackle. Winona wonders how to do a Lacan seminar when she's so excited about seeing Oasis this evening. Simon is lost in the ravaged landscape of Shostakovich. Paul will arrive in Toronto at 8 p.m.—people of earth, be warned. Benjamin is delighted there's a health-food book called What Would Jesus Eat? David is is-ing. Frank is always sunny in Philadelphia. Emma just overheard this line over a Pumpkin Spice Latte: Her Hitler hairdo is making me feel ill. Cooper's cat Kairos is hairballing again. Aaron is acting in Akron. Debbi is drunk in Dublin. Hank is horrified he just found a music file for Hoobastank on his computer. Daniel is amazed his amazing daughters are amazingly older than they were 5 minutes ago. Rhonda is sad today is her last as a redhead. Winona is asking herself when a vowel followed by a double consonant and a y is ever irregular. Heather remains happy. Thurston has a theory there are only two responses to life: love or fear. Owen is out of ideas. Alex is obviously a confused sad little person with confused sad little dreams who is NEVER drinking again. Dennis wishes the local weatherman would show some pessimism. Virginia is sitting vigil with a dying family member. Polly sometimes finds interesting artifacts in her desk drawers. Sara wants a goiter for Christmas. Rita is peeling red tape off her life. Brenda researches broken ribs. Ethan is hating on Damien Hirst. Genkei has been granted a four-hour reprieve. Kami is seriously and unapologetically addicted to Josh Groban's Christmas CD. Gabriel is about to embark on Phase II of his love-handles augmentation procedure. Lena is so oh-Q-Tip-how-I've-missed-you! Jim just finished updating his Facebook status. Jeff loves jet lag and irony. Vicki's sinus infection meds are making her crave Bruce Willis movies. Myla wonders when her son will figure out that bobbing for apples isn't going to be easy with no front teeth. Ripley is almost positive he just got cold-called by a phonesex company; that's the official story, anyway. Rhonda is now a blond. Rusti wants you to be her little spider monkey. Lily has learned that hockey pants are called breezers, but remains afraid to ask why. Tom is sitting with his left index finger up in the air to stanch the bleeding. Wallace just heard the animals say: We got the funk. Cooper: the hairballs are, for want of a better word, polychromatic. Tia believes in torture, not as a political tool, but as a lifestyle choice. Wes is watching some boring author boring everyone with her boring personality on Book TV. Polly just found an alien hair in her library book! Herman got out of work the hard way: by flying down his front steps onto his back. Trish is trying to figure out why her @tab variable is not working correctly. Alisha: If I were a Disney princess, these presents would wrap themselves—and sing while they did it. Tori: Dear Coworker: I love you to death, but your frog-noise text-message notification is making my brain melt. Kirby has cancelled the holidays—sorry, kids. Roger was enlightened once, but was able to see his way past it. Sofie suspects this year has really been all about next year. Chris is creating something with his legs. Nina thinks knight errantry is H=O=T. Luke is confident he is really the ghost of a lethargic butler. Heather is happy. Jim wonders if a narwhal could take a panda in a fight. Benjamin is like: KFC for dinner … damn you, clever product placement on The Wire! Randy is contemplating an article title: In Praise of Candied Ham. Wayde is waiting for the dream life to begin. Sam was there, but currently is here. Vicki is now friends with Advil Liqui-Gels®. Sara did not just send you a gift. Fred is not on fire, but thanks for asking …

We Are at the End of the World

THE ONE WHO WORKED at the dry cleaners loved photography. Click, whir: the world shaped by him. Every weekend he wandered the involved city, snapping his own reflection in windows. Bakeries. Boutiques. Sex shops. You could never make out his features because they were always hidden behind the flare of flash. He developed weather disappearance, a disease that gradually subtracted him. In the end he became a faint dusty scent tanging what had until then been his hospital room.

He died and next he realized he had been translated into part of the optics board inside a stranger's digital camera. Each time the stranger took a person's photograph, the subject's face appeared to the man inside the camera as it would at the instant of the subject's death. The man couldn't tell where the person was, or how he or she would die. All he saw was his or her face— sometimes frightened, sometimes peaceful, sometimes agonized, sometimes oblivious to what was happening to the body to which it was stuck. It was not the eyes that interested him, but the mouths. Something always floated out of them as people transformed into objects.

Flickering hummingbird ghosts.

Gifts from the dead.

Rising, the tiny birds sang. At first the man thought he was listening to a collective form of weeping. Then he grasped he was listening to stories, only very fast, and very many at once.

The one about the potter's field beneath Washington Square where the bones of more than 20,000 indigents and yellow-fever victims lay until one afternoon in 1849, when the parade ground there was reworked into the site's first park, and bones dissolved into the ambient noise often mistaken today for traffic.

The one about the young woman in Barcelona who, having slit her own throat in despair, returned as a perpetually sour taste at the back of her faithless boyfriend's tongue.

The one about the lonely American ex-pat who died unnoticed in a shack overlooking a wide white Mexican beach. His body bloated two weeks before vanishing, only to come back years later as an inconsequential island, aswarm with raucous curassows, floating hundreds of miles off t

The one about Elin, my wife's aging aunt, who last weekend during our visit to Palm Springs, deliberately sat apart from us by the painfully blue pool after her daily dialysis, hunched in a chair facing her own reflection in the sliding glass doors two feet away while the rest of us fought to make small talk about nothing I can remember. *Don't you just love these mornings?* her husband asked out of nowhere. Elin's thin sandy voice lifted above her chair back. *I don't love anything anymore*, she replied. My wife, her uncle, and I carried on examining the way light sparked off the pool surface, waiting for anything to happen.

one about ,

                                                 painfully

chair
glass

               just love

above   *don't*

                                     light sparked

                waiting

.

Billness

THE DAY DOESN'T FEEL EXTREME: the fifty-two-year-old man with a gray goatee and gray uncombed hair standing at the kitchen counter, buttering his toast, looking idly out the window at the woman maybe in her thirties, forties, leaning over her sink rinsing morning dishes in the small steel-blue house across the gravel driveway.

How the woman's dirty-blond hair frizzes around her face so the man can't make out her features.

She either doesn't notice him or doesn't care he's looking.

Her skin is puffy, the complexion of cement dust—the kind of skin, it occurs to the man, the paper mill across town will give you if you wait around long enough to let it.

Deb, the man's wife, saying behind him in her pink terrycloth bathrobe: You want some juice with that, hon, it's in the fridge.

The man knows without turning that Deb is resting both elbows on the Formica tabletop, eating an onion bagel with cream cheese, mouth open a little, that she probably has some smeared below her lips. The man doesn't answer, just looks idly out the window, buttering, mind blank as the sheet splashed across the clothesline in the backyard.

For now his name is Bill.

Chained to the fender of Bill's pickup with the camper in its bed, a dog barking and barking as if it has just realized it is going blind and there's nothing to be done about it.

Dawn. An overcast sky. Ashen light a drab glow, patches of grass still frosted white beneath trees like inverse shadows.

Bill stowing the last of his camping gear, battening down his two-man raft, walking around to the driver's side where Deb is waiting. It is Friday. Bill will be back Sunday afternoon. It is November, his solo weekend. It isn't like Bill is angry with her or whatever. It's just that sometimes taking her in it strikes Bill he needs to get away for a couple days, maybe go fishing. It's like, he tells her if she starts giving him that look, when you're watching one channel on the television and sometimes you just need to flip to see what's on the others, even if you're already enjoying the one you're watching fine.

Unchaining the dog, walking around to the passenger's side. Jake, an oversized golden lab, beginning to barkwhine. Bill releases Jake's collar, patting the seat.

Thatta boy, he says. Thatta boy.

Jake bounds up, circles so happy-clumsy he thunks down into the space between the seat and the dashboard, bounds up again, thunks down, tail thumping the seatback and the dashboard like a ruffed grouse's wings thumping.

Bill's father worked in the paper mill nearly twenty-five years before his lungs started going bad. Hell, he told Bill when he used to complain about the bitter stink as a boy, smell gets in your hair, clothes, bedding. A week, you don't even notice it no more. But Bill did notice it. He noticed it almost every day of his life: sickly sweet and sulfurous. It made everything he ever ate turn sour in his mouth.

One day at dinner his father began coughing up amber sputum laced with blood. He was forty-eight. Two months later he was retired.

Bill hoisting himself into the cab, settling, leaning forward, inhaling the tang of dead cigarette smoke and ripped car seats and wet dog fur, key turning in the ignition.

After he left the mill Bill's father would sit in his La-Z-Boy recliner mornings, afternoons, evenings, green oxygen canister by his side, clicking through channels on the TV, drinking Cokes and eating Jujyfruits. When he felt flush he would smoke a cigar.

He felt flush at least once a day.

The engine catching on the third try, radio blaring to life in the middle of a Taylor Swift song, and Bill takes this as a sign, knows everything will come out right now.

How Bill's mother, a small wiry Swede with skin like the crust atop cream-of-mushroom soup when you let it stand too long, cradling a sack of groceries in one arm, would glare at her husband sitting there in that recliner, point to his pregnant belly with her free hand, ask: You feeding that thing again?

The pickup backing out. Bill's house receding as Bill remembers in a brief incandescence how as a kid he would watch the middle-aged men and women towing their oxygen canisters behind them through the Lewiston Center Mall as if they were pets on leashes.

Two bedrooms, one bath, tan siding, roof the hue of acorns, front steps bright green Astroturf.

In high school Bill's first wife, Hollie, had known other boys, almost married a guy in his mid-twenties named Dale who worked at Albertson's and wore wife beaters and worn-out cowboy boots and owned a faded red Mustang convertible. Only Dale got that Karen Nehler knocked up and got hitched to her, so Hollie started paying more attention to Bill. Eventually she promised she'd marry him if he had a solid job with good benefits. Bill decided to become a male nurse because he liked medical shows on TV, the idea of all those mysterious tubes hooked up to a single human body. He liked how people had to depend on you or else they'd die.

Easing onto highway 95, dropping south, Bill reaches over and rubs under Jake's jaw. Jake leans into his hand, buries his nose in it, sniffing, gooing Bill's palm with clear dog snot. Bill wipes it off on his jeans. The pickup shoots across the bridge over the Clearwater, dry brown bluffs lurching up and down all around.

Dialing through radio stations Bill isn't interested in locating good songs. He just enjoys the physical action of dialing. It's like he's creating his own tune from other people's tunes. It's like he's a kind of musician.

The program at Lewis Clark State College was harder than he thought it would be, but he applied himself, knew he wasn't dumb as his teachers told him, ended up taking two extra years to finish because he was working at the Stinker Station down the street, and then opened his eyes to find himself on the eleven-to-seven shift at the hospital up in Moscow, find himself getting into Hollie's pants, and next they were married, Hollie had become a police woman, and she looked awesome in her uniform, only it turned out she never stopped seeing other guys. She got a pea in the pod. Bill remembers her sitting on the toilet in their doublewide with the home pregnancy test extended toward him in her hand, like: What the fuck is this? They didn't want to think about it so they took care of things. When Dale and Karen filed for divorce, Hollie told Bill in the note he found taped to the bathroom mirror upon returning from work one morning that Dale had always really had her heart and she was sorry and she hoped maybe they could all three be friends someday.

I am greatful to have had you in my life, it concluded. *I guess I will be seeing you. —XOXO*

If the weather had been different that day, would other things have been different, too?

Three hours, and the pickup jouncing along unpaved road hugging a river in the mountainous central part of the state boiling with rapids, pines slurring the edges of his vision.

Bill met Deb almost ten years after Hollie because the Starbucks he was sitting in happened to be full that afternoon and they had to share a table. He'd just gotten around to convincing himself he wasn't going to meet anyone again, his luck was just bad and that was okay, so he didn't have much to say to her. Except next he saw how Deb was kind of chubby and insecure and all he needed to get her going was smile a little and say something about the coffee, which arrived too hot, and that's what he did. He decided he liked the way Deb turned out to be uncomfortable around other men, the way she cut her fake black hair short in a what do you call it, a bob, so it made her appear even bigger than she was, the way she wore a silver nose ring, circumference of a pinkie tip, width of a thick human hair, that promised surprises that weren't going to be very surprising.

After his father's death Bill's mother moved into a cramped apartment over in Asotin that had a view, she insisted, when the trees lost their leaves, of the Snake River winding through the arid landscape below. Bill and Deb, who had moved into their own house, the one with tan siding and roof the hue of acorns, visited once a week. Bill's mother baked them tuna casserole, Bill's favorite. Deb, who worked as a sales clerk at the mall, brought two-dozen homemade peanut-butter-and-chocolate-chip cookies in the same pretty red tin each time. She drank diet cola and, pretending she was just nibbling while they watched sitcoms and talked about nothing Bill could remember the next day, always ate at least half the cookies herself.

Three and a half hours and the pickup rolls to a stop in a clearing ten feet from the surging whitewater. Bill slides out, stands there, eyes shut, palms on hips, face tilted skyward, breathing and listening, Jake bounding out behind him, commencing a maniacal investigation of the vicinity.

Next thing, Bill is going to work: tugging the raft from the back of the camper, dragging it down to the sandy shore, returning to the pickup for his knapsack, fastening it to the floor of the raft with colorful bungee cords, thinking: This is where mistakes happen. This is where things can go wrong.

How he learned to love Deb.

How he learned to call her Baby Girl, just like she liked.

He did rounds, poked his head into small pistachio rooms lit by single translucent nightlights, checked on sleeping patients, strolled down nearly dark corridors, over the years developing plantar fasciitis, which made the bottoms of his feet smart all the time like he had torn a tendon.

At his station he did a little paperwork, watched a little homemade porn on the web, checked the road conditions and weather report in winter because whatever.

Once or twice a week everything would fly apart, the call from the incoming ambulance arriving, or maybe a patient limping through the front doors asking anyone who would listen for help: car accident, labor pains, allergic reaction, broken ankle, sprained wrist, asthma, chest pains, ear infection, flu, knife wound, overdose.

Bill always secretly hoped for more.

When things happened he didn't have to think too hard. The doctor on duty would step in, begin telling him what to do. More and more, Bill came to like that feeling.

Building a fire pit out of good-sized stones, collecting kindling, thicker branches, deliberately dousing the whole with a full can of lighter fluid, chucking in the match: the *whoomf*, the firecloud bursting and contracting into fierce crackling.

For lunch: two hotdogs on a stick, a can of Heinz beans, two bottles of Fat Tire beer.

One of the hotdogs, half the can: Jake's.

Leaning against a tamarack, mesmerized by the river's churning. Jake gruffing to himself, settling down beside you. Finished eating, you lift his head, cradle it in your lap, stroking it, thinking about nothing, letting the sounds of the rapids rush through you.

A crow passes directly overhead. You can hear the *whuff whuff whuff* of its wings flapping.

The sky: a chilly lint gray like a massive field of grimy snow only upside down.

Eight years old Bill is out back listening to his father, shotgun in hand, saying about the pair of flickers that have bored into the eaves of their house: You got to be patient, boy. Watch 'em. They take the same route every time. All you got to do is study the situation some, think about what they're going to think about before they think about it, then *wham*.

How Hollie did stuff in bed that Deb didn't want to learn. How you came to like that feeling, too. How sometimes you looked at your wife across the table at the Red Lobster on your monthly date night and it seemed to you as if she didn't have a thought in her head, so you'd ask her what she was thinking, and she'd say nothing.

Lewiston, Idaho, in July: a hundred-degree blankness that made leaving your car seem as if you were leaving your soul.

When Bill rises again he is shimmering with resolve. The speed of his actions startles him. He heats water in a pan, gets out his razor and handheld mirror from the camper, erases his gray goatee and uncombed gray hair. He has never seen himself bald before. Examining the results it dawns on him he looks like someone he doesn't know. He tilts the mirror at various angles, tilts his head, in order to see himself from different vantage points. His pate feels cold and so he returns to the camper for his black knit cap. Tugs on an extra sweater, tan with brown elbow and shoulder pads, zips up his camouflage parka, eases on his heavy black gloves, eases off his heavy black gloves, double-checks his pocket for the roll of bills, eases on his heavy black gloves.

Kneeling, he calls Jake over, rubs his head, lifts him wiggling in his arms and nosing Bill's face and kissing him with his dog-breath tongue. Bill soothes him with his gentle voice, staggers down to the shoreline, and heaves him in.

Jake's head swirling momentarily in the frothing rapids, spinning around and around like a honey-beige ball, and then just the rapids.

Bill standing on the shore, waiting for something else to occur, then dragging down the raft the last few feet to the water, tossing in his wallet and keys, the water grabbing it out of his hands.

Bill rifling through his camper to make sure he has everything and walking along the frozen dirt road through a light snow, gloved hands in his pockets, head lowered, concentrating on his Billness flecking away behind him with every step he takes, legs cold, then less cold, then warmer.

He becomes Pete for a while in Boise because he has always wanted to be a Pete, but in Pocatello Pat sounds better, and in Laramie sometimes Chris, sometimes Butch, and there are whole weeks when he doesn't have to be anybody at all. That's when he simply becomes the fifty-two-year-old man in his mind, and the fifty-two-year-old man hitchhikes to Jackson Hole via Cheyenne and Casper, because he has always wanted to see Jackson Hole, and, although he is impressed by the jagged snow-capped mountains surrounding the place and huge arch made of antlers at the entrance to the town square, he hitchhikes back into Idaho and then up to Bozeman, where he finds work doing odd jobs at a local gas station, buys a used sleeping bag and a 1978 Chevy Malibu with a rusted roof from a guy with three and a half fingers on his right hand, and sleeps in the backseat in the parking lot because his boss tells him he can be night security guard, too, if he wants.

It doesn't cost much to wake up, wash in the restroom, sweep here, mop there, help someone hoist this or that, wander Main Street to Seventh and then south to Cooper Park and beyond to the University so he can look at the cute girls before wandering back.

It doesn't cost much to keep his deodorant, toothpaste, floss, and new razor in a brown paper bag under the front seat. He takes up smoking again, stops. Buys an ounce of pot, throws it out. Sees his name in the paper twice, photo once, then that goes away.

It doesn't cost much to eat cereal for breakfast, lunch, dinner: Frosted Flakes, mostly, but sometimes Apple Jacks, Froot Loops, or Cocoa Krispies.

But the fifty-two-year-old man has to back off when it starts feeling as though that shit has begun gelling his blood and his stomach burns in the middle of the night and he starts getting ideas, so he switches to Pop-Tarts, then to bags of pre-popped cheddar popcorn, then to bags of ranch-flavored potato chips.

Baked.

Like, for instance, how freedom is what you do with what's been done to you.

The weather starts turning harsh in early December, wind swirling in hectic with snow, so he crosses back into Idaho again, drops down into Utah, driving at night, sleeping on logging roads and at rest stops during the day, but for no more than two hours at a spell. He passes through Salt Lake City, where he sells his car to a vet back from Iraq, then hitchhikes to Provo, Nephi, where he buys another, a silver 1986 Hyundai Excel for $625 from a twenty-year-old caddying at the Canyon Hills Park Golf Course, searching for warmth and finally locating it south of Cedar City in St. George, whose red rock cliffs remind him of the westerns he used to watch as a boy on the black-and-white set with rabbit ears in the living room while snacking on Chef Boy-Ar-Dee frozen pizzas.

Bonanza. Rawhide. Gunsmoke.

He lands work doing odd jobs at an apartment complex where the manager cuts him a deal on an unrented studio in the basement, decides he enjoys moving boxes, washing windows, painting walls, tearing up old carpet, but most of all getting down on his hands and knees to scrub filthy bathrooms until they smell like chlorine because that's where things begin one way and end another, decides he enjoys being neither here nor there at any particular minute, neither this nor that, enjoys living in the space between words.

Death Valley Days. Broken Arrow. Bat Masterson.

The vet told him over beers the night he bought the fifty-two-year-old man's car about his buddies and him being on patrol at the outskirts of a congested market in Karbala one morning when someone just stepped out of the crowd and raised a pistol to the neck of the last guy in the patrol and fired and then just stepped back into the crowd.

The fifty-two-year-old man wakes at three one morning in February, gets into his Hyundai, and drives to Las Vegas because he can't sleep. He takes a room in a cheap motel away from the action, gets a lift, drifts into the MGM Grand, where he admires the lions in the large glass cage inside the casino area, into New York, New York, where he eats a slice of pepperoni pizza and rides the rollercoaster, into the Venetian, where he floats in a gondola past cafés and beneath bridges on an artificial canal, watching the artificial sky seventy feet above him turn cloudy, turn clear, turn midday, turn miraculous pink-and-blue sunset spray.

Afterward he enters the casino, orders a double scotch, and takes a seat at a roulette table. In fifteen minutes he has lost half his money. In twenty-five, two-thirds.

Stepping out onto the sidewalk he realizes it is already the next day. Someone hands him a flier with photos and lists of specialties by local hookers. The fifty-two-year-old man balling it up as he strolls south, air already hot and thin and dry. He drops the flier on the sidewalk when he thinks no one is looking, the fountains at the Bellagio jetting to life as he passes: twelve-hundred nozzles, forty-five hundred lights, two-hundred-forty-feet high, Sinatra's *Fly Me to the Moon* surging on the massive sound system.

Then he doesn't leave his motel room for two days. Sitting naked in the chair by the wall-unit that makes the place smell vinegary, watching game shows and eating Cheese Puffs, then pretzels, then Cheese Puffs again.

He drinks Mountain Dew. He drinks Pepsi. He drinks Jolt.

He is driving north through the most nondescript desert he has ever seen, flipping from radio station to radio station. He is in Nevada. He is in Idaho. He is listening to Hank Williams. He is listening to Pearl Jam. It is still dark and he is in Lapwai on the rez twenty miles from Lewiston. He pulls into the grocery store parking lot, his car the only one there. Leaving the keys in the ignition he strolls out to the highway and raises his thumb.

When there is no answer he moves around the back of his house, knocks, waits, knocks, then walks in, wipes his boots on the mat, continues into the kitchen where he takes a seat at the Formica-topped table.

Thirty minutes, forty, Deb shuffles in for breakfast.

She is wearing her pink terrycloth bathrobe. She hasn't put in her nose ring yet, combed her hair.

She fetches up in the kitchen door, studying him. He feels his Billness trickling back in behind his forehead.

Outside the sudden violent blueness of the sky.

Just These Minutes

THEN MY LITTLE MAN NATHAN reaches over at the breakfast island and starts wailing on little Caleb and little Caleb goes down like a cement sack and them only two years old with Crispix and milk everywhere and it's Sunday which I'm sitting there with my bacon and sunny-side-ups trying to enjoy myself a little on my day off at the base with the Cowboys game in the living room and those two going at each other all week long which I've been telling them to stop that shit but sometimes they get a mind of their own and Nathan is all over Caleb now punching kicking slapping and my Johnny Junior he's six just stares into his Froot Loops like they about to make an important announcement but Ella who's four my beautiful angel she's been picking at her Cinnamon Toast Crunch like the very idea of food bores her but when that first squeal goes high in the kitchen her head pops up and she's all like *smack him smack him smack him* that's my princess and off her chair she hops and Caleb does that thing you see stunned people do after they been ninjaed which they sort of wobble in place wondering what the fuck just happened instead of thinking for instance about fighting back which means Nathan already has him in a headlock which I'm guessing it surprises Nathan how fast he gets the upper hand which he don't know quite what to do with once he got it but I'm sitting there trying to listen to the game but I've pretty much had it with them two and so I nip off half a stick of bacon I'm holding kind of daydreamy between my thumb and forefinger and reach over for my camcorder which it's a nice little Canon PowerShot TX1 with a 10x optical zoom optical image stabilizer technology and I'm thinking well maybe it's about time just to let them get it out of their system so I suggest to my little Caleb who my little Nathan has in the headlock and is now punching kind of in the neck *he started it son so you hit him back you man up don't be such a fucking pussy* only Caleb's being a fucking pussy and can't even I don't think hear me because he's screaming like a little girl and Ella is out of her chair and around the island and two feet away from them shouting encouragement which the tiny blood vessels on her forehead are sticking out and her tiny face this excited pink-purple and so cute it hurts which Johnny Junior is still trying to hypnotize his Froot Loops and Nathan is sort of paralyzed trying to work through what to do next and I recommend he consider each of his limbs a weapon and explain how each can prove to be a valuable asset in hand-to-hand combat which Caleb all wimpery begins trying to kind of turtle out from under his brother's grip which Nathan's on him like hot gum on a cold sneaker so I recommend to Caleb not wanting to play favorites *get the fuck up you're not even TRYING* which Ella who is always one to keep focused on a mission returns to her initial proposal shrieking into Nathan's ear *smack him on the head smack him on the head* which information Nathan apparently finally begins to digest because he gives it the a try with some limited success and it don't get no more adorable than a couple blue-eyed towheads working out their differences in the kitchen which is the moment my ex would start going all liberal on me which is when I would tell him that he didn't know what the fuck he was talking about because he lived in a fucking *bubble* selling those fucking Toyotas and why the fuck doesn't he just once try out a nice sunny weekend in fucking Fallujah because then you can get back to me about which I'm guessing the judge seemed to agree with me because who has custody of the kids if you know what I mean and who lives with his fat momma in Omaha plus in all honesty what we got ourselves here is a teaching moment which I'm somehow already out of my chair and recommending to Caleb *quit trying to go all French on me* because it's getting a little you know embarrassing what with my own son attempting to pussappear but then *bam* Caleb all shrieky and snuffling sort of shrugs off Nathan and regains his footing wiping his nose and being all stoop-shouldered and snot-thready but the little guy still doesn't seem to quite get it because Ella from the sidelines counsels Nathan *push him down push him down push him down* which Nathan immediately does which Caleb regains his footing again and all shrieky and snot-thready tries shuffle-whining away which I go to Nathan *every time he tries to run you beat him up you hear* because he got to learn and the last couple days Caleb's been all sneaking up on his brother when he's sleeping on the couch in front of the TV and noogieing him in the arm and laughing and running away to lock himself in the bathroom before Nathan even knows what's what or like last night when him and Nathan got into it and Caleb goes rapidly faggot on us all by grabbing his brother's wrists and dancing him around and kicking him in the nads which you know what goes around comes around which these hit-and-run deals you just got to stop because sometimes you got to take off the dress not that we didn't have our good times him and me back in high school before he started fuglying up with that beer gut driving out to the Oradell reservoir from Hackensack and shedding our clothes and gliding into the black lake with the pickup's radio playing back on the shore and the sound of our breathing side by side and arms lapping the water which now Caleb is back on the floor snivel-screeching and covering up and it's just so fucking sad that my own son can miss the point so profoundly which I hear myself going *how do you like it huh come on get up get up* which is when Johnny Junior steps into the frame pushing past Ella and sort of squats there trying to pull Nathan off Caleb's back and I'm like *NO YOU DON'T* which I reach out and grab him around the waist and yank him out of the scene explaining *your brothers've been itching for this shit for days you just let 'em turn up the volume* and Ella shouting *keep going keep going keep going* and pretty soon the door to Johnny Junior's room slams shut and Nathan and Caleb are at it again which it's really something to see how much energy you have when you're that age and then Caleb does one of those things where he kind of explodes but he's facing the wrong way and so only gets a glancing smack off Nathan's ear which simply pisses Nathan off more who starts with the sissy-kicking again which is when the Cowboys pull off what must be this sweet play and in the living room the crowd goes wild but I can't see nothing from where I'm at and somehow one of Nathan's fingers pokes up Caleb's nose briefly which doesn't quiet things down any but Caleb is sort of pressing himself into a corner now over by the fridge covering his face with his hands and attaining this impressive steady high note of pure anguish while Nathan karate-chops him in the back and sides while Ella stands maybe one inch away from Nathan's ear sort of leaning into it squealing *harder harder harder* and I'm just starting to remember my breakfast back on the breakfast island because the whole kitchen is like stunned with the smell of bacon which I catch a glimpse of the blood on Caleb's upper lip that maybe comes from his nose and maybe mouth which gets me to thinking how great this all will look on YouTube because it's both educative and hilarious at the same time which when I see the blood though and it isn't a lot or nothing just kids being kids I fig-ure it's probably time to pull the plug which is what I do letting the cam-corder roll for a little bit longer can't help myself before going *okay boys that's it we're done and dusted* which I'm guessing they probably had enough for now anyway which I'm thinking if a day can start this well you never know where it's going to go.

An Arsonist's Guide to the Empire
[Draft #1]

DIR. SENNA CELLO. CINEMATOGRAPHER: Lea Con Lens. Cast: None.

One can We can all Anyone who Who doesn't remember Andy Warhol's *Empire*, an 8-hour weighing in at 8- the 8-hour film of the Empire State Building shot from a fixed angle perspective from evening to next early next morning? Like Joyce's *Finne*

Like Pynchon's *Gravity's Rainbow*, Warhol's *Empire*, an 8-hour experimental film of the Empire State shot from a fixed perspective from one evening to early the next the following mourning morning is one of those most-talked about and least-seen artistic works of the 20th century. Made between 25 and 26 July 1964 from 8:06 p.m. to 2:42 a.m. at the offices of the Rockefeller Foundation on the which floor 40th? 41st? of the Time-Life Building, 16 blocks from the Empire State, Warhol's silent flick silent movie tour de Warhol's silent tour de force this sentence is too long. *Empire* begins commences with a shot the first shot The film opens with a white screen and, as the sun sets, a foggy nebulous a vaporous image of the iconic New York edifice materializes appears emerges. Its exterior floodlights on its exterior come to life ignite and flicker ignite, flickering on and off for the next six and a half hours. In the penultimate next to last reel they cut off and the remainder of the movie of what we see takes place in nearly complete total darkness. During three of the reel changes filming recommenced before the lights in the filming synonym room were switched off, making the ghost faces of director Warhol and cinematographer Jonas Mekas momentarily conspi visible in the reflection of the widow.

Empire was Andy Warhol directed and Lithuanian-born filmmaker Jonas Mekas worked as cinematograph Filmed at 24 frames per second, *Empire* is screamed screens at 16 fames. Although only six hours and 40 minutes were shot, it became becomes eight hours and five minutes when. The duration turns converts translates transmutes transforms you wouldn't believe English is my first language seemingly at first glance evidently apparently ostensibly insignificant events like a lone bright rising balloon bright balloon rising fact check into dramatic instants into the tense the taut space of drama, leading critic Pauline Kael to quip once: *I loved it, but found the plot twists a bit difficult to follow.*

Yet *Empire's* importance lies not so much in its execution as in the tremendous adventu audacity of Warhol's probe Warhol's project, which itself, which translates that translates art-mockmaking from material into philosophical act situation operation. For it asks viewers to commit to a nearly impossible challenge

to commit to the performance of deep of practiced attention in order, as Warhol once said, to watch, as its creator once said, to watch time go by, as the poster boy for Pop Art which this isn't an example of so why mention it commented I think fact check. For it asks it's For it asks its synonym to commit to a nearly impossible performance of attention—to watch, as its maker as Warhol commented, time go by, I think. Abbreviated condensed no abridged showings were never Warhold Warhol never allowed abridged showings. Supposedly the film's

Purportedly the film's very unwatchability of the synonym was of its *raison d'etre* good god its rationale as was its lack of script and goal to elevate the banal the prosaic the commonplace to the level of visual fetish.

In *An Arsonist's Guide to the Empire*, filmic provocateur Senna Cello both celebrates and deconstructs jesus i hate undoes? complicates? the terms of OK complicates Warhol's celebrated controversial undertaking. With the unblinking wrong adj. eye cliché synonym of performance artist and cinematographer Lea Con Lens, Cello shoots the Empire State from precisely the same viewpoint Warhol did. Yet instead of Yet rather than producing eight long ours hours and five minutes of floodage footage by slowing down a six-hour-and-40-minute shoot, Cello begets ack creates an eight-minute-and-five-second video by speeding up six-years-and-four-months of filming. By taking only a handful of frames each day, she, like Warhol, invites the audience to fuk to focus on how time happens at us— yet in a completely different way and for completely different ends different purposes goals intents missions motives motives? What arrives on the screen is What we witness is a reminder

The film reminds the viewer, not only of the velocity of the contemporary, but also of a stunning critic word alert investigation into the unaccounted for, ghost already used haunted come on silenced presences, jesus, existential aporiae god no just shoot me. While Cello's attempt initially strikes one strikes you strikes the viewer as

is imminently watchable,

it soon becomes apparent its punt

is imminently watchable, it soon becomes obvious that unwatchability is its real synonym, no matter how much attention one you we the viewer may verb into the effort the attempt the act no the effort no the act.

What you don't see, over and over again irremediably, is how the Empire State was completed ahead of schedule, taking 3400 workers on site at a time a mere a single year and 45 days to build. One doesn't You We don't see how it cost $24,718,000—a figure far below budged budget because of the Depression. We

You don't see the five people who died on the job: struck by truck; dropped down elevator shaft; hammered by hoist; skidded off scaffold; blundered into blast area. Because they're not there, because you can't find them, because

You can't get out of your mind that there are 1860 steps leading from street level to the 102nd floor. Seventeen million feet of telephone wire running gushing surging running through the place its walls the walls of the place the place's walls the walls. Can't lose sight of the fact that that edifice that skyscraper that erection gahhhhhhh that tower was the tallest in the world between its completion in 1931 and 1972, and then not, and then the 15th tallest and how, at 10:28 a.m. on 11 September 2001, it once again became the tallest building in New York.

What you don't see is how the Empire State's distinctive Art Deco spire was originally designed to act as mooring mast for dirigibles, a vision out of some H. G. Wools fever dream, but proved to be something, proved to be impractical, not to mention something else, dangerous, that's it, dangerous due to as a result by virtue of powerful updrafts caused by the size of the building itself that no one had forecast how dumb is that, and

as well as the luck lock lack of mooring lines tying tethering the other end of the craft to the ground. How more than 30 people have committed suicide by leaping by sailing by bounding from the building nice alliter. Perhaps most famous is poor 23-year-old Evelyn McHale, who plummeted to her dearth from the 86th floor observation deck on 1 May 1947, smashing into a U.N. limousine that had just pulled up to the curb below. A few minutes litter photography student Robert Wiles took a snapped a picture a few minutes later of her unnaturally uncannily intact corpse body better thuddy word. In the shot, McHale looks peaceful, composed, as if she's merely catching 40 wanks. The result ran in the 12 May issue of *Life* accompanied by the caption The Most Beautiful Suicide—a photo appropriated by none other than one Mr. Andy Warhol himself for use in his infamous hebejebe Death and Disaster series composed of repeated shocking images of car crishes, race riots, murmurs, electric chairs, and nuclear outbursts

In other wards, the complete history of New York over the course of the last six yours years and four mouths thrums in thrums through appears in *An Arsonist's Guide* by that history's very un-thereness. The viewer sees

You see everything you can't see. The 2006 blizzard and blackout: AWOL. Yankee pitcher Cory Lidle's plane rimming into that redbrick apartment building on the Upper East Slide. Rats ruling the West Village KFC/Taco Bell while Bernie Madoff smirkily unravels on TV screens around the country. Flight 1549 bobbing serenely as a rubber ducky on the Hudson. The olive-green sleeping bags, translucent blue plastic sacks, tents, tarps, whooping placards, makeshift kitchens, spidery lengths of orange bungle cord, and frowzy protesters overflowing Zucotti Park. But you also see what was never there in the first place to begin with originally: disproportionate Fay Wray in King Kong's 1933 clutch, Henry Fonda ordering bomber pilot Dan O'Herlihy to use the Empire State as ground zero for his atomic egalitarianism in 1964, Tom Hanks and Mug Ryan hyperbolically wheeling around through zipping up and down that concrete superstar in 1993.

All art, Senna Cello argues, argues Cello, this latest unWarhol claims, is a conversation across time and space. All history is misremembered story. And all trauma will eventually become nostalgia for that which never existed. Which is to say *An Arsonist's Guide* is serious busyness. But that hasn't stopped certain Italian crickets

certain Italian critics from proposing from demanding Cello return her Cannes prize for what they assert charge allege is a "pedestrian prank," a "ludicrous one-liner perpetrated on an unsuspecting pubic," while one of the French cognoscenti has gone so far as to make the annoyingly loud case that Cello's *chef-d'oeuvre* is nothing more than "pococurantism parading as art" what the hell does pococurantism In Amman curious theatergoers were yelled at by humorless protesters. At the London premiere little people dressed as pee-wee Empire States zigzagged through the line of befuddled ticketholders. And still the small audiences turn up keep turning at arthouse and museum showings new word, suggesting that viewers will be arguing about this one for as long as there are synonyms, even as its most upsetting legacy will remain the fate of Cello herself, mysteriously murdered only a week before its premiere in her native witzerland.

Why, When It Dreams Our World,
the Lobster Is Not a Telephone

LOB•STER *—N. ANY OF VARIOUS large, edible, marine, usually dull-green or gray, stalk-eyed decapod crustaceans having large, asymmetrical pincers on their first pair of legs, one used for crushing and the other for cutting and tearing; the shell turns crimson when cooked. Origin: before 1000; Middle English* **lopster**; *Old English* **loppestre**: *literally* **spidery creature (loppe** *spider +* **–stre –ster).**

Tonguing what she worries may be her too-big front teeth, Lola knuckles up her glasses on her nose and leans forward to watch the lobster maneuver over the backs and heads of its friends in the unembellished tank in the restaurant foyer. The restaurant is dark and velvety, the lobsters' claws rubber-banded shut in bright yellow. Occasionally the one in question slips down among the others, gropes up, continues its fumbling advance which, Lola thinks, isn't really the right word. Her tongue feels freshly scraped with a popsicle stick. She decides to read the crustacean's gestures as an expression of courage and so chooses it for dinner.

> *The female lobster carries live sperm for up to two years. She may opt to fertilize her 3,000 to 75,000 eggs (each the size of a pinhead) at any time during this period.*

At dusk in the Brazilian rain forests, *forelius pusillus* ants defend their homes by spending nearly an hour kicking grains of sand into the entrance holes until they blend in with the surroundings. Each evening anywhere from five to twenty-five workers remain outside to finish the job. Cut off from their colony, they die by morning. This is the first known case of suicidal sacrifice in the animal kingdom that is preemptive rather than a response to immediate danger, Finn, Lola's boyfriend, thinks as he shakes himself daintily and zips his fly in front of a urinal in the men's room at the Lobster Pot.

As with the snail, crab, and shrimp, lobster blood is a clear fluid. When exposed to oxygen it turns blue due to the presence of copper-laden hemocyanins within.

I dip into the neighborhood supermarket on my way to the lab to pick up a Snaggy Scree candy bar for lunch. I'm not watching my diet. I've never watched my diet. Waiting in the checkout line, I notice my wife, or perhaps a woman who only looks like my wife, at the seafood counter. It's her boyish hair, her short muscular body type. But her back is toward me so I can't be certain and there's a full length of supermarket aisle between us. This woman, who may or may not be my wife, is talking to a heavyset guy with a shaved head and wooden plug earrings sizeable enough I can just make them out even at this distance. Initially I assume he's an employee. I assume my wife or the woman who resembles my wife is asking him a question about, say, the catch of the day. Yet their exchange is lasting longer than I might have expected and the heavyset guy with the shaved head and wooden plug earrings is smiling more diligently than I might have imagined an employee would be smiling at an ordinary customer, female or not. Observing them from my position, I try to remember what my wife said she was planning to do today, piece together her itinerary.

The baby lobster swims at the surface of the water for its first twenty-five days. Only one percent will make it to the bottom.

Lola met Finn in Thompson's lab two and a half months ago at the beginning of the fall semester. Four afternoons a week they float among a small Sargasso Sea of other graduate assistants. Over an unfolded lobster Lola mentioned in passing to Finn this evening would be her birthday. Finn, warming up the nearby CrustaStun, spontaneously asked her out in a manner that didn't precisely sound as if he were asking her out, but rather as if he were making an ironic statement about the concept of asking out someone who might or might not have been Lola. Still, now they're here in the midst of this date, or what appears to be a date, although neither would admit that's what it is, because it isn't, exactly.

> *Inside the lobster is a green goopy substance called tomalley, which fulfills the functions both of liver and pancreas.*

Dalí's famous assemblage *Aphrodisiac Telephone* is composed of a black rotary dial phone with a colorful plaster lobster stretched across its handset. The artist made four copies in 1936. One appears at the Dalí Universe in London, a second at the Museum of Telecommunication in Frankfurt. A third is owned by the Edward James Foundation, and a fourth exhibited at the National Gallery of Australia. Perhaps in oblique response to questions concerning the piece's origins, Dalí writes in his autobiography, *The Secret Life*: *I do not understand why, when I ask for a grilled lobster in a restaurant, I am never served a cooked telephone; I do not understand why champagne is always chilled and why on the other hand telephones, which are habitually so frightfully warm and disagreeably sticky to the touch, are not also put in silver buckets with crushed ice around them.*

> *Lobsters are related to spiders. Both are arthropods (i.e., invertebrate animals with jointed limbs, segmented body, and exoskeleton), although each belongs to a distinct subphylum: spiders, arachnids; lobsters, crustaceans.*

Over breakfast my wife mentioned she would run several errands this morning. I recall the event itself, the vigor of coffee in the air, the gray-white sunlight blanching the room, but I can't remember any specifics. It's perfectly feasible one involved a brief trip to this supermarket. It's perfectly feasible one didn't. My wife, or the woman who resembles my wife, is conspicuously not pushing a shopping cart or carrying a shopping basket. Nor is she holding a cheerfully packaged product. Instead she is talking to the guy with the etc. The teenage girl with long pink hair and silver tongue stud behind the cash register hands me my change while focusing her attention almost exclusively on my neck. I contemplate strolling over to my wife or perhaps to her double and the guy with whom she is speaking in order to say hello but, before I'm conscious of having made a decision, I'm outside, across the icy November parking lot, hunched behind the wheel of my car, heater whirring, speed dialing her number on my cell phone.

Bisque: *a creamy, highly seasoned soup of French origin, classically of puréed crustaceans.*

The, you know… Britney Spears, progressively uncomfortable, prompts the host of the cooking show, *Celebrity Cuisine*, on which the pop singer is appearing in the hopes at least on her manager's part of reversing some of the damage done by Vanessa Grigoriadis's recent *Rolling Stone* cover story entitled *The Tragedy of Britney Spears*. It's all, you know, pink and gooey, like Thousand Islands dressing? What do you call it again? Britney tries to laugh, but the attempt comes out a chirp.

When boiled, lobster blood turns into an opaque whitish gel carrying no discernible flavor.

Although Finn is, Lola feels, too tall for her by a good six inches, too doughy and pale (he reminds her of an overweight Kevin Federline), not to mention uninteresting in that excessively diligent graduate-studentish way, she nonetheless discovers herself unexpectedly here on her twenty-eighth birthday, leaning forward to better witness her meal's slow scrabble across its fellow meals' exoskeletons while she waits for Finn to reappear from the restroom. Lola ticks the tank glass with her fingernails, focus gliding gradually away from this particular armored being and toward her job four afternoons a week assisting Thompson investigate how lobsters in general perceive sound. They can, it turns out, produce low-frequency rasp-like ones by contracting a small sonic muscle in the base of the large antennae. What's odd, though, is that they don't tend to do so during social interactions, but rather when resting alone in their shelters, as if they preferred talking to themselves rather than to other lobsters. Each time Lola raises one from its tank she can feel (not hear, but feel) the vibrations emanating from it. The sensation is reminiscent of her cell phone set to silent, only organic. At first it creeped her out, only she's slowly forced herself to get used to it. The spiny (as opposed to true) lobster possesses an organ at the base of the second antennae that makes a variety of noises, including scratchy ones (during aggressive encounters or when predators are nearby), slow rattles and flutters (when secluded), and pops (when wandering around solo outside its shelter)—which is even odder, the more you think about it, since neither the true nor spiny models sport the functional equivalent of ears, which is to say they mustn't sense sounds like humans do, if at all, which for some reason puts Lola in mind of how everyone's voice comes back to them outlandish when heard on a recorder. This is because when you speak sound energy spreads in the air around you and reaches your cochlea through your external ear by air conduction while also traveling from your vocal cords and other structures directly to the cochlea. The mechanical properties of your head enhance the sound's deeper, lower-frequency oscillations. The voice you hear when speaking, then, is this combination of sound energy carried along both pathways. If you listen to a recording of yourself, however, the bone-conducted pathway of your normal hearing voice is eliminated, and hence you hear only the air-conducted component in unfamiliar isolation, which, naturally, always strikes you as someone else talking—as if you were listening to a stranger repeating exactly what you've just said with no other purpose than to make you uneasy.

The teeth of the lobster are in its stomach.

Ectrodactyly, also known as Karsch-Neugebauer or Lobster Claw Syndrome, is a rare congenital deformity of the hands, feet, or both where the middle digit is missing. While it is an inherited condition, it can skip a generation. The Stiles family has been afflicted with it for at least two centuries. In 1805, William Stiles was the first in the lineage to display it. He was followed by Jacob Stiles (1843-1932), Elisha Stiles (1880-1935), and Grady Stiles Sr. (1912-1988). The latter became a sideshow attraction among firewalkers and cannibals from darkest Africa beneath gaudy banners in towns across America, and, shortly after Grady Franklin Stiles Jr. was born in Pittsburgh on July 18, 1937, his father added him to the lineup. Grady's stage name was The Lobster Boy. His condition was so severe it prevented him from walking. He therefore employed a wheelchair in public and in private learned to use his hands and arms for locomotion. The result was he developed extraordinary upper body strength. He married twice and fathered four children. Two of them were born with variations of ectrodactyly. Although the siblings were from different mothers they sometimes toured together as The Lobster Family. Grady was popular as a friendly, outgoing teratoid. Behind the scenes it was a different story: Grady was an abusive, jealous drunk. He frequently bullied, threatened, and beat his wives and children. Even so, no one could have guessed that

Lobsters often resort to cannibalism in captivity.

At dusk in his suite at the Bellagio hotel Kevin Federline is killing himself. Propped among a white silk pillow garden that is his vast heart-shaped bed, he watches with interest as his hand delivers powdery blue pill after powdery blue pill to his mouth while he feels himself become increasingly smudgy. Kevin wears nothing except a pair of black Emporio Armani stretch cotton briefs with their signature oversized waistband. Across the room on the 103-inch plasma flat screen, Brit's video *Someday (I Will Understand)* is set to continuous play. Among his popping, chewing, and swallowing, Kevin mouths the lyrics: *Nothing seems to be the way that it used to…* But he isn't really thinking about his ex. He would like to be, but he can't get his brain to pay attention to what he would like anymore. It's industriously recalling a conversation he had earlier in the day with that cute guy with amazing abs who served him his fourth piña colada with chilled lobster down by the pool. The guy had had this bad case of the hiccups and, when Kevin said something humane-yet-funny to make him feel a little less self-conscious, the ab-man (who was, it so happened, double-majoring in biology and studio art at UNLV) went off on this sort of weird riff about how the *hic* of hiccups can at times be caused by blockages or lesions that crimp one of the nerves controlling respiration and are an evolutionary hand-me-down from amphibians. These nerves relay brain signals that induce a muscle spasm in the throat and chest, causing the epiglottis to shut the windpipe. The sharp inspiration and obstructing of the throat—the *hic*—are a legacy of tadpole-like creatures pumping water into their mouths when breathing through their gills. As they inhaled water, the creatures' glottis clamped to prevent fluid from entering their lungs, which were used for respiration on land. *Step into the words*, Kevin mouths to himself, although if you asked him he'd say he wasn't making a sound. *Step into the noise.*

The question of whether or not lobsters experience pain is unresolved.

But my wife doesn't answer and I don't leave a message on her voicemail. I hang up and sit behind the wheel, heater whirring, reach forward, turn off the engine, swing open the door, slide out, slam the door, and track back across the icy November parking lot into the supermarket. The teenager with the long pink hair and silver tongue stud behind the cash register recognizes me and is vaguely disconcerted by my reentrance. I'm disconcerted, too, because when I turn up the aisle at the end of which my wife, or the woman who could be said to bear a close resemblance to her, was speaking with the heavyset guy, both are gone. I amble over to the seafood counter as if I might be checking the produce and hang around examining the lobsters until a man behind the counter asks if he can help me with something today. I tell him no, no, thank you, just looking, which may or may not sound faintly peculiar to him. Although late for the lab, I strike off down another aisle, up another. On the PA system, a gender-ambiguous voice announces a special on Annie's Homegrown Organic Cheddar Bunnie Crackers. Regularly $4.99, we always-hopeful shoppers are informed, for the next two hours these yummy, crispy snacks made with organic wheat flour and real cheddar cheese will be on sale for a not-to-be-missed $3.39.

When in danger, the lobster propels itself backward quickly by curling and uncurling its abdomen. A speed of five meters per second has been recorded.

Across the table from her Finn's mouth is moving but Lola isn't taking in what it has to say. She's concentrating on how she's feeling bored, only not bored in a drab, monochromatic way, but bored in an agitated, fizzy one, and how she's been feeling like this ever since Finn and she took their seats, fluffed their napkins, and opened their menus. Fortunately there's enough ambient restaurant commotion to keep her semi-distracted. So she forks a lettuce leaf, purple onion sliver, and maybe a radish crescent, and slips the conglomerate between what she fears may be her too-big front teeth. Finn laughs at something he just said. Instinctively Lola, studying her empty utensil, musters a laugh's dead grandmother as well. When she raises her head, chewing, she notices over Finn's left shoulder one of the chefs step from the kitchen to the lobster tank, where in a magician's graceful gesture he extracts one of the fidgeting (and, Lola knows, vibrating) crustaceans within. From her perspective the lobster balances momentarily on Finn's shoulder like a parrot on a pirate's. Then both chef and crustacean disappear through shadows and swinging cherry-wood door. *Happy birthday*, Lola thinks to herself, glum, staring down at her salad glistening with too much oil and vinegar. What? Finn asks. Huh? Lola asks, glancing up on a wave of adrenaline, caught.

It isn't unusual for the lobster to live more than 100 years. Scientists believe it may exhibit negligible senescence, or very slow or inconsequential aging, in that it can effectively exist indefinitely, barring injury, disease, or capture.

When in 1978 Grady's oldest daughter, Donna, fell in love with and became engaged to another teen, Jack Layne, Grady sensed he had begun losing his grip on her. Furious, he demanded she call off the wedding. Donna refused. Grady broke things and ordered his daughter from his mobile home. The couple ran away. Several weeks later, from an undisclosed location, Donna called Grady from a phone booth and, lying, told him Jack had gotten her pregnant. She explained they had to get married now. Grady's voice dissolved into remarkably poignant fatherly concern. He told her he forgave the couple their transgressions and urged them to return home to Gibsonton, Florida. It was time to put differences in the past. They deserved a nice family wedding among kin. Donna and Jack returned and set about preparing for the festivities. The night before the ceremony Grady drank himself into staticky grayness, rolled up behind Jack while he was watching television, and shot him three times in the head. Despite openly confessing to the murder and showing zero remorse at the trial, Grady ended up serving no time. His lawyers argued that, since the American prison system was not equipped to deal with a disability like Grady's, confining him to a penitentiary would be tantamount to cruel and unusual punishment. The Lobster Boy was therefore let off on fifteen years probation. One might assume this was the end of Grady's bizarre st

This quick backward movement is known as Caridoid Escape Reaction.

Nearly half an hour late to the lab now, I give up looking for her and, glum, aim for the sliding doors again. Stepping into cement-colored light I catch sight of a black Acura with shadows flickering inside parked down the row of cars to my left. A couple seems to be going at it inside. From my viewpoint one of them—the one in the driver's seat, the one closest to me—appears to be the heavyset guy from the supermarket. Given his position and mine I can see neither his face nor his partner's. Curious, I veer toward the car. As if on cue the driver quickly disengages, rearranges himself behind the wheel, and commences backing from the space. Next the Acura is crawling away from me through the parking lot and I'm following. I pick up my pace—from stroll to jog, jog to run. The Acura maintains a several-hundred-foot lead and, up ahead, eases into line behind three other vehicles waiting to enter traffic on the hectic main thoroughfare beyond. Waving, I spring off the curb in a sprint. My right foot comes down funny on a patch of ice. I hear the moist pop. Head all fluttery, my lower half drops out from beneath my upper.

The American lobster did not become a popular food until the mid-nineteenth century, when New Yorkers and Bostonians developed a taste for it. Prior to this, eating lobster was considered a mark of poverty, the food of indentured servants.

Bisque? offers the host of *Celebrity Cuisine*, an aproned Michelin Man with meticulously trimmed two-day stubble and really loud personality. Britney senses her focus loosening as she sorts through the flowchart behind her forehead. Her eyes go blank for a heartbump and she realizes some idiot with nothing better to do in East Orange, New Jersey, or West Valley, Utah, is probably pricking up his ears and reaching forward to hit *record* on his Apple TV. Within an hour these eight stupid seconds of her life will be posted on YouTube. Within two they'll be metastasizing across the web. By tomorrow morning, Whoopi, Joy, Elisabeth, and Sherri will be analyzing them on *The View* with some bald psychologist hawking a degree from the University of North Texas who knows precisely jackshit about who Britney is, but doesn't mind gaining a little airtime anyway by pretending he does. By tomorrow evening Jay and Dave will be cracking jokes at her expense as though the pop singer has no purpose in the greater world than to function as those withering asswipes' punch lines. By next week there will be some photograph from the clip tucked away somewhere near the front of *People, Entertainment Weekly*, and *In Touch.* And yet standing here right now, staring off into space, thinking about these things, Britney understands there's nothing she can say or do about any of it, which only forces her to stare off into space and think harder, because once one of these machines is set in motion, once the media judges you a cultural gag, nothing you can say or do will seem other than gaggish. Once the verdict has been passed by the hive mind, you're boned because that's when They stop seeing you as some fucked-up human being in the cosmos just like everyone else and start seeing you as a spectator sport … a-and pretty soon a hundred shit-grinning paparazzi are hiding behind the next tree or in the next car or over the next twelve-foot-tall protective wall, biding their time till you put on a couple pounds, or drive away from some goddamn Starbucks with little Sean Preston in your lap, or shave your head because, well, why the hell not, who the fuck is it harming anyway?—so They can make some quick cash taking hurtful photographs of you and igniting hurtful rumors about you … and the truth is pretty soon you've stopped remembering any of the good things people have said, any of the caring ones, although there are plenty of them, seriously, like for instance all you have to do is check out the blog at www.britneyspears.com or the message board at www.britney.org … yet all that ends up sticking inside your skull like some fistful of thistle are the little evil phrases that fly at you over Facebook or from the latest snarky London tabloid—*Brit waddled around the stage lip synching and looking scared*, a-and *tour de farce*, and *Britney's vagina made another bid for freedom Tuesday*—that make you want to evaporate into the very air surrounding you.

> *Because of the ambiguous nature of suffering, most people contending lobsters have this capacity employ argument by analogy—i.e., they hold that certain similarities between lobster and human biology or behavior warrant the assumption lobsters feel pain.*

Dalí created *Aphrodisiac Telephone* with the specific intention of aligning the lobster's genitalia with the end of the phone into which one speaks because for him crustaceans and telephones carried robust sexual connotations.

> *Spiders are related to angels in the sense that both species possess eight limbs (angels commonly having two sets of wings) and profound hope.*

On the evening of November 29, 1992, Grady was sitting in the living room of his mobile home, drinking Seagram's 7 and watching sitcoms on television with his wife, Mary, and stepson, Harry, when a faint rapping arrived on the windowpane. Grady paid no attention. Perhaps he didn't even hear it. But the noise was a secret signal for Mary and Harry to leave the house. A few minutes later they made excuses and slipped out. A few minutes after that Christopher Wyatt, the seventeen-year-old Mary and Harry had hired for $1500, entered and with the grace of a magician shot Grady three times pointblank in the back of his head with a .32-caliber handgun. The Lobster Boy was fifty-five years old. Upon her arrest Mary explained to police she had orchestrated the killing to escape years of physical and emotional abuse. While the jury acquitted her of first-degree murder and conspiracy to commit murder, it found her guilty of the lesser charge of manslaughter. She was sentenced to twelve years in prison. My husband was going to kill my family, Mary told the judge in her statement.

I believe that from the bottom of my heart. I'm sorry this happened, but my family is safe now.

In some restaurants, lobsters are chopped open and served while still conscious and struggling. This is referred to as live sushi.

Finn watches Lola festively crack open her crustacean's claws across from him and wonders how he ended up at this table this evening. Lola is nice enough and all, in a sort of large-toothed, mousy graduate-studentish way, except Finn never would have asked her out if he hadn't felt really sorry for her. It's her first semester at the U., after all, and she doesn't know many people because she tends to be super quiet and keep to herself and give off these vibes of über-confidence which themselves give off vibes of unfathomable insecurity. Somehow the idea of her spending her first birthday here alone just seemed all messed up. And so, right in the middle of all the other graduate assistants, Finn heard his voice asking her out. It sounded to him as if a stranger had begun speaking through his vocal cords. Now he's worried she's probably imagining this date thing to be something other than it actually is, and he's forehead-slappingly aware that he isn't helping the situation any. Listen to him rambling on like some frantic putz, packing the dead space between them with dumbass anecdotes like he always does with women he doesn't know very well. Plus he already has a crush on Ayako, the cute girl in his biochemistry class who's shy in a sexy way and always seems to have the correct answer when called on and started wearing those oversized furry boots months before anyone else. Finn has been wanting to ask her out for ages, only he can't stand the thought of her eyes starting to unfocus over his shoulder when he pops the question, shocked that a nerd she's never even noticed before would have the testicular fortitude to do such a thing. Lola dips the white chunk of meat impaled on the tip of her fork into the butter, swirls it, and slides it between her greasy lips, which, Finn can't help remarking to himself, she's forgotten to wipe for a while now. Somehow her gesture recalls this concept he learned about in anatomy class yesterday, the Uncanny Valley Effect, which takes note of the fact that, whereas cartoonish or abstract human figures in video games, say, draw immediate empathy from viewers, animations that appear very similar to humans, but not identical, provoke a sense of unease. Everyone knows how freaky it feels looking at stilted eye movement or a lip twitch on the part of an otherwise fairly hot anime character. If represented on a graph, that uneasiness translates into what's called an Uncanny Valley, a deep dip, register of the observer's comfort level plummeting pretty much to zero. That's why roboticists, for example, aware that they can't create robots that are indistinguishable from humans, build robots that don't look like humans at all—big, clunky, 1950s versions of the future. Which is also why the work of cosmetic surgeons often yields a version of the Uncanny Valley Effect on the part of viewers. All you have to do is think about Joan Rivers or Michael Jackson. Their countenances exist at the exact same location on the Graph of Unease as that occupied by the handicapped, the disfigured, and the sick, because, most likely, your genes get worried at the sight of them that their genes won't reproduce well. Which is simply to say people should wipe their mouths more often, right?

> *Just before cooking, one can place the lobster in a freezer for five to ten minutes to immobilize and sedate it. Alternatively, one can employ the CrustaStun. Designed by a British barrister, this electrocution device humanely kills the crustacean within five seconds by sending a 110-volt shock through its body. The CrustaStun is available online for about $4,000.*

When I die, it will have been here. It will have been in Las Vegas, Nevada. It will have been in a heart-shaped bed in Las Vegas, Nevada. It will have been in a room on the thirtieth floor of the Bellagio in a heart-shaped bed in Las Vegas, Nevada. When I die, it will have been with a video of my ex singing to me and not singing to me from across the room. It will have been imagining the curtains on the far side of which is a picture window overlooking the fountain in the middle of an eight-acre lake. It will have been following an afternoon listening to a beautiful boy tell me about the amphibians within us beside a pool the color of these sleeping pills. It will have been inhaling the chlorine scent of my sheets, thinking about that pool. It will have been a little past three in the morning. It will have been in nothing more than some Armani stretch cotton briefs. It will have been taking note of the *shush ... shush ... shush* of my own breath diminishing. Observing how my tongue feels scraped with a popsicle stick. Watching the ceiling through my closed eyelids because opening them will have come to insist on the same strength as swimming the English Channel. When I die, it will have been wondering what I am doing now, and now. It will have been wondering how I am doing what I am doing and what I am not doing. It will have been wondering about this thing, this blue flame that has begun encircling my right hand. It will have been wondering about whether I am actually watching it, or only believing I am watching it when in reality I am doing something else entirely. It will have been wondering what my burning hand could mean, if it could mean anything at all, what it could point to or might become. It will have been wondering about whether I am thinking about this or not thinking about it as I study my hand withdrawing from me across an ocean of blackness, a tinier and tinier blue glow, how it must at some point have ceased to become my hand and become someone else's because it is so far away, how it is shrinking and shrinking until

> *In February 2005, a review of the literature by the Norwegian Scientific Committee for Food Safety concluded: It is unlikely that lobsters can feel pain. The report hypothesizes that the violent reaction of the crustaceans to boiling water is simply a reflex reaction to noxious stimuli.*

Maybe Lola is in her apartment. Maybe it is Thanksgiving or Christmas and maybe she is alone and maybe her new boyfriend is waiting for her in the living room, glass of red wine in his hand. Maybe we know his name and maybe Lola is sitting beside him. Maybe there is a fireplace. Maybe she is standing at the Formica counter in the kitchen, slicing tomatoes and mozzarella for a salad she is preparing. Maybe there is music playing. Maybe it is something classical. Maybe Lola is examining her hands at work, how they look older, more chapped, fingernails splitting, than she would have imagined. Maybe she is humming along with the classical music under her breath, oblivious of the lobster rotating in the microwave behind her. The lobster is scrabbling to face the oven door. The lobster is looking out. The lobster is ticking at the glass with its claws, politely but insistently, as if it might not already have Lola's attention.

Table of Contents

THE (STRONG) MAXIMUM RASHING PRINCIPLE

THE (WEAK) MAXIMUM RASHING PRINCIPLE

APPENDICES

Appendix A
Transcripts (1):
Mind ghosts fail into language.

Appendix B
All right, Jane, get into the carriage.

Appendix C
Moist Global Verges (Hope's maps).

Appendix D
Problematics of the Larynx:
The branks, the butter, the dark, the rippers, the bent fork (& belief in an afterlife), the bent fork (& lack of said belief), the cat's paw, the hare's foot, the pear, the frightening thought of seeing through the idea of yourself to yourself, the knotting, the strappado, the blankness, the fully-realized conceptual project appearing precisely like the world, the roses, the awry, the array.

Appendix E
Memory Breaths (Hope's marginalia).

Appendix F
Black is the best color, for it goes with everything.

Appendix G
Transcripts (2):
Look at blueness drown in beauty.

Appendix H
No. Plum. A hue.

LANCE OLSEN is author of more than 20 books of and about innovative writing, including the novels *Theories of Forgetting*, *Calendar of Regrets*, and *Nietzsche's Kisses*. His short stories, essays, poems and reviews have appeared in hundreds of journals and anthologies, such as *Conjunctions*, *Black Warrior Review*, *Fiction International*, *Village Voice*, *BOMB*, *McSweeney's* and *Best American Non-Required Reading*. A Guggenheim, Berlin Prize and N.E.A. Fellowship recipient, he serves as chair of FC2's Board of Directors and teaches experimental narrative theory and practice at the University of Utah. Visit him online at <www.lanceolsen.com>.